DeDe:
Freshman Year

Robyn D. Jones

Archway Publishing books may be ordered through booksellers or by contacting:

Archway Publishing
1663 Liberty Drive
Bloomington, IN 47403
www.archwaypublishing.com
1 (888) 242-5904

ISBN: 978-1-4808-8925-5 (sc)
ISBN: 978-1-4808-8926-2 (e)

Library of Congress Control Number: 2020904474

Print information available on the last page.

Archway Publishing rev. date: 05/18/2020

Chapter 1
Summer Break

It's not easy being me. I'm fourteen, about to go to high school, and I'm invisible.

I've always been like one of the boys. I walked, dressed and even played like a boy. I didn't have any girls that were my friends. For some reason, I never really fit in with girls. And for some reason, I didn't care.

My brother Ty's friends, were my friends. I went with them everywhere- from each other's houses to hanging out at the basketball court after school. I spent hours watching his friends act like they were going to be the next up and coming rappers. They would create rhythms with their mouths like Dougie Fresh or Biz Markie and spit lyrics that none of the hottest artists could touch. Since I was the only female, they always had me sing the hook, which I thought always made their raps sound a thousand times better.

Ty's fun was my fun. I loved my brother so much. It didn't matter what he wanted to do, I would do it. We spent school nights and weekends playing video games. I was often the target when his friends wanted to feel good about themselves. They would often underestimate me, thinking that they would win every time they came over and demand to play a vicious game of Madden football or the latest 2K NBA game. Little did they know that when they weren't there, I would spend hours practicing under another alias so that I could beat them.

But my favorite game was basketball. Ty and I would play every day on the single basketball hoop my parents bought for the driveway. We would play day and night, winter, spring, summer, or fall! It didn't matter as long as I was playing. Although everyone would come to play at our house, there was nothing like playing ball in the city.

Every time I visited my grandmother's house, Ty and I would walk four blocks—passing two corner stores, three liquor stores, and one storefront church—just to get to the court that sat behind what used to be the old rec center. Years after the city closed the center, it became an abandoned shell of a building that drug addicts used for shelter when the weather kept them from roaming the streets.

Every time I stepped on the court, I always took in the scene. It was like that moment in the movies where the athlete became one with the court before they played the best game of their life. I took a few deep breaths even though the air was filled with the stench of trash and the smell of crabs and fish from the street vendors. The court was my sanctuary. It didn't matter what it looked like or smelled like, being there just took me to another place in my mind.

The white and orange paint was peeling off the backboards and rims. On the far side of the court, the rim was bent down like a limp branch on a tree after a storm. The nets were tattered or totally removed, but it never stopped the best of the best in the hood from playing.

I was just as good if not better than any dude in the neighborhood. I dominated the court. I knew I was that good because whenever we would choose teams, I was always one of the top two players to be picked. Everyone that played treated me like one of the boys, and that was exactly what I wanted. I knew in order to become the best, you had to play with the best. They elbowed, pushed, and tripped me. They tried anything to keep me from scoring. But I was better, smarter, and faster.

Don't get me wrong, for years my mom tried really hard to give me "girly" things to do. From the ages of four through eight, I was in ballet with a guy named Earl, who loved tights more than I did. And my gymnastics career, from ages nine through eleven, came to a screeching halt when my newly grown hips and breasts made a series of flips feel more like flops.

Then basketball happened to me. I fell in love from the first time my dad put that ball in my hand. The smell of the leather, the feel of each groove giving me the perfect grip—it was truly a magical connection. Some may call it fate, but I knew that basketball is my destiny.

Now, I live and breathe basketball. My best games have always been against my brother. He taught me, challenged me and pushed me to do my best every time I stepped on a court.

Now Ty's graduating from high school and going off to college. From now on, I will be on my own. Just me. Ty was not just my brother, he was always my best friend. It's going to be so strange. I have to practice basketball—and learn about life and get insight on boys—on my own. Everything is changing- I'm going to high school, Ty's not here and now I feel even more... invisible.

The Move

I was packed and ready to go. We were living in one of the craziest parts of Baltimore City. But needless to say, it was home. I didn't think I would miss being one of nine people in a four-bedroom row house. The row houses in Baltimore looked small on the outside but were very spacious on the inside. Once you started adding people and personalities, the space that seemed big, got smaller and smaller.

I knew when we moved, I wouldn't miss the broken sidewalks in their many shades of gray. The cracks sometimes made it hard for us to find a place to play double-dutch. I wouldn't miss the daily newspapers, empty bottles of liquor, candy wrappers that you could only buy from candy lady that lived two doors down and fast food scraps lining the gutters from block to block. There weren't many leaves in the gutters or floating around because the only tree along the sidewalk was in the middle of the block-hence why they called inner city neighborhoods concrete jungles. I didn't think I'd miss the old men outside the corner store playing checkers or dominos, cussing out loud and talking trash to throw off their opponents. Nor would I miss the group of five to ten dudes hanging out on the opposite corner shooting dice and fighting when someone grabbed the money too soon. I didn't think I would miss not being able to leave my front stoop or playing kickball and making up cheers in urine-infested alleys. Those memories slipped away as if into a distant past when we pulled up to the new house.

My mouth fell open. The house was huge; it was beautiful, and it was mine, mine, mine. I was so excited, I jumped out of the car before my dad could even put it in park. I ran across the perfectly cut green lawn to the front door.

My arms and legs were shaking because I was so happy. My heart pounded as I watched my daddy put the key in the lock and open the front door; I wanted to push through like the linebacker on the Baltimore Ravens, but instead I closed my eyes and waited.

When I opened them, I was surrounded by tall white walls, a long staircase that looked like the entrance to heaven and a chandelier that hung right over my head. Each crystal in the chandelier sparkled as it reflected the light from the window on to every wall that surrounded it, like the rainbow prism experiments in science class.

You could tell Mommy was happy. She had no words and she always has something to say. A tear ran down the side of her face as she gave Daddy the most endearing and romantic kiss on the cheek.

I ran up the stairs and tripped just a few steps from the top. I was embarrassed but all I wanted was to see my room.

My room was made for a princess. Everything was beautiful azure blue with white accents. My dad knew exactly what I loved. I had a queen-size bed with a sheer canopy hanging over it. It had four huge pillows and a large, fluffy down comforter. I've never felt any material that was so soft. I felt like I was lying among the clouds.

The sheer curtains that covered my bay window matched my comforter perfectly. I've seen bay windows on the TV shows where the rich people lived in mansions and had servants for their every need. But I never even dreamed I would have one of my own. The bay windows on TV were big enough for one person to sit in and maybe a pet dog, but my window seemed much bigger. I could cuddle up, read, or daydream all day long in my window. And the window had the perfect view. I could see all the houses in the cul-de-sac. I could watch the sunrise every morning. At night, I could admire the stars and the moon.

On the far side of the room, there was an L-shaped desk in the corner. On one side, there was plenty of space for me to do my schoolwork. There was a calendar on the wall and a small library of my favorite books. I'd been totally hooked on history and poetry books for the last two years. On the other side of the desk, there was a brand-new computer. The desktop was fully loaded with a flat screen monitor, a webcam and a printer.

To the right of my desk, I glimpsed a closet door. I opened it to reveal a huge walk-in closet. It was like an additional room had been added on to my room. There was a place to hang my clothes, fold my clothes, and arrange my shoes. Daddy knew how to hook up my room. But it wasn't always like this ...

The First Move

Three years ago, we were living pretty well. We lived in the suburbs. We had a nice three-bedroom brick house. Everyone had their own room. We always ate well, and we wore nice clothes. Of course, things were not always brand-named, but we still looked nice. I went to Catholic school because my mother believed I needed more of a challenge than what they were giving me at my neighborhood school. And twice a week I took gymnastic classes. The other days I spent my afternoons with my brother and his friends hanging out. My brother went to public school, played in the marching band, and for the most part was on honor roll. He didn't tell his friends how smart he was because it made him seem not so cool. But his grades and extracurricular activities looked good on his résumé and his college applications. My dad worked in the insurance industry as a salesman, and my mom was a manager at a local retail store. Everything seemed like it was going well, but it really wasn't.

When I was eleven, my mom decided to go to college. I was proud of her because she had put her dreams on hold to raise my brother and me. She deserved a better life. My dad, being the great man that he is, took on the task of being the sole provider until she graduated. It seemed like he was handling it quite well. He took care of everything. He worked every day, bought groceries, took me and my brother to all of our activities, and made time to tuck me in and say prayers every night.

Then out of the blue, *wham!* My dad's employer let him go. I didn't understand. He had spent his whole life, since getting out of the military, as a salesman. He had the best numbers and clients loved him, and yet the company didn't need him anymore.

My dad was from the old school: they did everything by hand or by using common sense. He was a hustler; he always made things happen. He had the gift of gab, and now he was being replaced by some young guy just out of college who did the same thing but knew how to incorporate the latest computer software programs.

When my dad lost his job, things began to change—for the worse. In the beginning, we did not notice a change in routine, but some nights you could hear my parents arguing and praying about what we needed to do. One Saturday morning, my parents called my brother and me downstairs for a family meeting. As we sat around the kitchen table, they told us that they had come to the decision that we would live with my grandparents until they could get back on their feet. My dad still wanted me to stay at my school and for my mom to continue to pursue her dreams in school. Being at my grandparents' house allowed him to look for a new job and save up for a new house. So sadly, we packed everything and moved to Grandma's. We left the only home that I had known since I was born.

It wasn't an easy move for any of us. My aunt Tina and her children were staying at my grandma's already. Aunt Tina, my mom's sister, had recently separated from her husband and also needed a place to stay. Altogether, nine of us were living in a four-bedroom row house. I had to share a room with Angie, my cousin, and my brother shared his room with the baby, Justin, Angie's younger brother.

It wasn't the worst situation, but it wasn't easy either. My grandparents didn't live in the best part of town. Years ago when they first bought the house, it was beautiful. All the neighbors knew one another. The streets were safe to walk wherever you wanted; but times definitely changed. Now many of the houses were abandoned. The boarded-up doors and windows were never a deterrent for the homeless drug addicts and rats to infest the empty homes.

My grandparents believed in taking pride in their home regardless of what the neighborhood looked like. We all had chores. No one was exempt. We cooked, cleaned, did the laundry, and took out the trash. And when all was done, we had fun. Angie and I used to play double Dutch with Tracey, our friend from across the street. We would constantly compete over who could jump the fastest. Angie would always win.

I used to love going to the corner store. Mr. Johnson (the store owner) had known my family for a long time. He was about eighty years old but was still very handsome. He had silver hair and a fit physique, but my favorite part of his appearance were his big, beautiful hazel eyes. Mr. Johnson would spend hours telling us stories about when our parents were young, and he would laugh so hard, he would spit all over us. Sometimes we thought dentures would come flying out!

One day on our way to the store, Angie and I heard a gunshot. Someone was trying to rob Mr. Johnson's store. I was scared. I grabbed Angie's hand and ran back to the house. My heart was pounding, and I was shaking. Luckily, Mr. Johnson was okay. Apparently, the robber sent a warning in the air signaling he was about to rob the store. Well, Mr. Johnson surprised him with a Louisville slugger. He knew how to defend himself from his training in the military. By the time the police arrived, Mr.

Johnson had duct-taped the man around his mouth and torso and left him on the front stoop to be picked up.

After that, the rules in the house changed. We were no longer able to walk to the store by ourselves. We could only sit on the front stoop. If we wanted to play, we had to go in the back. We hated playing in the backyard. The area was small and gated. Once my granddaddy parked his 1970 Lincoln Continental, there was only enough room for us to just stand and look at each other. The car was so long, there was no room in the yard to play tag or jump rope.

Our parents tried to explain that they were doing it for our protection but all I could see was them being mean. I thought the new rules were unfair.

Things were so bad that I was ecstatic when school finally started again. I wore a uniform every day so people couldn't tell that I shared clothes with my cousin Angie. During the summer, I found myself lying to people; saying things like "Oh, she just wanna be like me" or "Our moms went shopping together." I had a new excuse each time we both wore the same outfit within the same week.

My dad continued to drive me to my friend Tanya's house every morning just like he used to do. The school bus would pick us up from her house. Tanya lived in my old neighborhood. I never told her why we had moved. I was ashamed of the situation. Fortunately Tanya was a good friend and never asked.

School was school. I did pretty well; I was a B-plus student. My parents stayed on me hard about my schoolwork. There was no such thing as bringing a "C" grade in the house. If I did, I was immediately punished until the next grading period. And behavior was never a problem in school. I left that craziness for my brother.

Christmases were really hard. Although I knew by this time

that Mom and Dad were Mr. and Mrs. Claus, I still expected big boxes under the tree for me. I was apprehensive when it was time to make my list but proudly handed it to them. Their faces saddened with the thought that I might not receive anything on that list. I was torn. I felt bad for giving them a list that they might not be able to afford, but I felt that I had done everything they have asked of me at school and home and deserved a nice Christmas.

My parents did what they could. On the third Christmas at my grandparent's house, they were able to get me a couple of things off my list. I was happy until I saw Angie's father bring her everything she had asked for. I can't lie, I was jealous. I mean, this girl, a C-minus or D-plus type of student, who talks about her dad as if he's lower than dirt and thinks she's a know-it-all, and she gets more than me? Once again, life just seemed unfair.

Tensions started to rise. By the beginning of the New Year, Angie began to flaunt all of her new items. She would tease me and talk about how my dad didn't have a steady job, and that was why I didn't get anything for Christmas. One day she went too far, and I snapped. I began to beat her up. I couldn't stop. I could hear in the back of my mind everything she'd been saying to me for the last three years, and in that one moment I was going to make her pay for each and every time. I ran over to her and pulled her hair from behind to stop her in her tracks. She stumbled a little and I pushed her to the ground. I punched her in her stomach and face. And then I just kept hitting and scratching her until my grandma came in the room to break it up. When she pulled me away, I cried until I couldn't cry anymore.

And just when I thought life wasn't fair, my grandma showed me how unfair it really was. She gave me a spanking like I've never had before. I didn't understand why. Afterward she explained that fighting is wrong especially against family. Looking back, it's funny how old school folks "beat" you to let you know it's wrong to fight. Needless to say, we were separated, and I was put in the room with my brother and Justin moved with Angie.

My father came to my room a few hours later and had a long talk with me. He told me that I hurt his feelings because he never raised me to fight but he understood when I explained I was fighting for family honor, his honor. There was no way I was going to let her keep talking bad about my family. And if it happened again, I would do the exact same thing! He smiled and gave me a high five and a wink as if to say he was proud of me for sticking up for family and happy that I whooped her butt! I did promise that I would try my best not to let people make me upset like that again.

We talked for about an hour. Dad told me that finding a job was really hard for him. He struggled with odd jobs to keep the family going, but he promised that he would try twice as hard so that I would never have to fight on his behalf again.

That spring I completed eighth grade. I was in the top of my class. My parents' love, excitement, firm rules, and values made me realize that even though we did not have a lot of money, they loved me and did not need to compensate that with material things. My awesome grades and my athletic ability earned me a full scholarship to one of the city's best Catholic high schools. My parents were proud, and I was happy that I'd saved them the cost of my schooling.

At the end of the summer, my parents called another family meeting. I thought it was to figure out how to say farewell to my brother, who was leaving for college in a few weeks. Instead, it was to thank us for being patient the last three years and let us know that, thanks to Dad's new job, they'd been able to save enough money to move. Little did I know where we were moving ….

Back to the Move ...

Sitting in my bay window and staring into the sky gave me time to think about the difference that three years could make. I could appreciate everything that happened, the good and the bad, and sent God a simple prayer of thanks.

About an hour later my mom called me down for dinner. It had been a long time since it was just us. We prayed, ate, and talked. We talked about Dad's new job and Mom's college classes. Mommy was really excited to share her idea of wanting to start her own business. It sounded pretty cool. It sounded like it would be a lot of work to get it up and running- which meant more time away from the family. We were used to her not being around as much, so it was easy to congratulate her and give well wishes. And then the conversation turned to me.

My mom asked me how I felt to be going into high school. I told her I had mixed feelings, especially because I would be attending an all girls' school. I was excited and nervous. St. Augustine's was one of the most popular all girls' schools in the city. And did I forget to mention that it was next to an all boys' school, St. Andrews (major bonus)? All kinds of questions swirled in my head: *What is it like going to an all girls' school? Will the boys like me? Will I fit in? Will the boys like me? Was I going to be one of the most popular girls? Will the boys like me? Was I going to maintain my A-/B+ average? Will the boys like me?*

My dad could sense my discomfort with the conversation and changed the subject. We talked about the new community. He pulled out a map on his Ipad. He pointed out the swimming pool, the shopping mall, and all the other essential places we needed to go. I couldn't wait to explore!

After dinner, I went back to my room and started to unpack my clothes. I made sure that every item found its place in the closet. I was exhausted by nine o'clock. It was not difficult to fall asleep in my new bed. It was the first day of a new beginning. Thank you, Jesus!

The next few days were routine. I spent time helping my parents getting things straight around the house. I unpacked all my boxes and updated my social media pages. I added new pictures that I took of myself in the new house. I wrote my daily blog and read all my new messages. A few of my friends from my old school left messages. Their messages talked about how much they missed me and said the school year wouldn't be the same without me. It felt good to be missed, but I knew I had a new adventure ahead of me.

I spent a lot of time looking out my bay window. One day I decided to step outside to explore. I went to the garage and dug my bike out from among the empty boxes. When the garage door opened, I stepped out and walked my bike to the end of the driveway. There was an eerie silence. The wind blew lightly. All of my neighbors looked as if they were moving in slow motion. To the right of me there was an older couple gardening.

I looked to my left and *screech!* "You better not go to her. That's my girlfriend. I called her first!" There were these two little boys yelling at each other. They smushed each other in the face and wrestled each other on the front lawn.

"Don't mind the twins" I turned around. The voice came from this goth-looking girl. She had long black hair and wore a black shirt that was slashed all over, black leggings that looked like they were mauled by a cat, and a pair of tall black boots. She had a light brown tone to her skin and slightly squinty eyes. The mix of Asian and African American descent was beautiful. "My name is Ray. It's not short for anything. It's just Ray."

"Nice to meet you. I'm DeDe."

"So, you moved into the old McGuire house. They were nice people. They moved to Florida."

I really didn't care. I got on my bike, hoping she would catch the hint.

"Where are you riding to?"

"Just around the neighborhood. This is my first time out. I'll see you around."

"No, wait. I'll join you. I'll show you around."

"Okay," I replied hesitantly. I wasn't interested in gaining any new girlfriends. The last time I thought a female was my friend, it was my cousin Angie. And we all know how that worked out.

Ray came whizzing down her driveway on a skateboard. *This girl is weird!* She did a few tricks and came to a halt next to my bike. We looked at each other and started moving from the driveway to the street. Ray pointed out all the houses. She knew who lived in every house, their occupations, and their family history (divorces, crazy kids, drug addictions, all of it). She even included who to talk to and who to avoid. She made the neighborhood seem as crazy and filled with drama as those insane women on reality shows.

We turned down another street and heard some rowdy noise. There was a group of boys playing basketball. There were six of them. You could hear the trash talk, the yo-mama jokes, and of course the boasting about girls. I had to stop to get a good look.

"That's Tommy," Ray explained. "He's a sixteen-year-old spoiled brat. He thinks he's the man because he's the only sophomore that plays on the varsity football team for St. Andrews." *St. Andrews ... hmm*, I thought. Wait...*That's the boys' school next to my new one.*

I stared a little longer, and Ray continued to talk about him. "He's one of those all-season jocks. He plays football, basketball, and lacrosse. He's a smooth talker. He thinks he's God's gift to the female population."

Every time Ray opened her mouth about this boy, he sounded better and better. You could tell in her voice that she had some type of animosity toward him. Anyone could guess that the two of them had a past. It didn't matter to me. I just thought this Tommy boy was cute.

When I realized the noise had stopped, I noticed that the boys were watching us watching them. "What's up, Ray?" Tommy said. "Who's your friend?"

"This is DeDe. She just moved here last week."

"Well, hello, Ms. DeDe. I hope to see *you* around."

Blushing, I said, "We'll see." I smiled and started to mount my bike again. I began to pedal, knowing that Tommy and his friends were staring at me and my butt as I rode away. All I could think about was my no-brainer one-liner: "We'll see." *I couldn't come up with anything better to say?* I knew I had to think of something better for next time.

I was worried so much about the dumb words that came out of my mouth, that I paid no attention to the pothole directly in my path. The pothole was small enough that a car wouldn't have a problem driving over it without damage, but for a bike on the other hand, it could be quite detrimental. And it was.

I hit the pothole head-on. My mountain bike threw me forward, gracefully launching me into the air. I landed face first in the middle of the street. I asked myself whether I was dead. After long moments of silence, I heard the thumping of several sets of feet coming towards me. Thankfully, I was still alive. I felt a sharp pain in my ankle, and my face was burning. I didn't know if it burned because I was actually hurt or just totally embarrassed.

"DeDe, are you okay? Are—you—*okay?*" They rolled me over. I opened my eyes. I could see Ray, Tommy, and all of his boys. It looked like they were laughing until Ray pointed out that my face was bleeding. Tommy leaned forward and winked. "I told you I would see you again, but I didn't think this soon." He smiled. "Let me help you up."

I tried to get up, but my ankle couldn't hold my weight. I tried to hold back my tears, but at that moment, I just wanted my mom and dad. Tommy directed me to stay there. Ray stood next to me. "Girl, you are better than me because I would be so embarrassed." At that moment I wished could have run home, buried myself under my new soft blankets, and eaten lots of ice cream to make me feel better.

Just then Tommy pulled up in his sixteenth birthday gift: a brand-new convertible sports car. It was silver with black racing stripes. *Nice. I'm sure all the girls love it.* He and his boys helped me get in the front seat. Tommy jammed my wrecked bike in his trunk, and Ray jumped in the back with two of his boys. Fortunately, we were only a few blocks from my house, but the ride seemed to take forever. Damian, Tommy's best friend, asked me if I was okay. When I told him I was fine, he just busted out laughing. He described the entire event and did a reenactment of me meeting Tommy, trying to be too cute riding away on my bike, and then how I landed on my face. We all couldn't help but laugh. That boy was so silly.

We got to my house. Ray ran to my door and introduced herself. She told my parents what had happened. They came running to the car. Tommy went to introduce himself, but my dad rushed right by him to come to my rescue. Mom thanked them all and told them that they would take it from there.

My parents took me to our car and rushed me to the hospital. The doctor came into my room to tell us I had a hairline fracture in my ankle. The doctor put a cast on my foot, gave me crutches, put a bandage on my face, gave me some painkillers, and sent me home.

The next day I must have slept really late because when my mom came knocking on the door, the sun was already high in the sky. She announced that I had company. I looked at my clock and saw it was one o'clock in the afternoon. I couldn't believe I'd slept the morning away. Ray took one look at the bandage on my face and the cast on my leg and couldn't figure out whether to feel bad for me or to laugh at how it happened. We talked and laughed for a while. Ray said she'd noticed how my dad pushed Tommy aside to get to me. I told her that he was just worried about me. But I knew the truth. Daddy has never trusted and never will trust *any* boy around me…

Daddy's Trust or Should I say Mistrust Issues

When I was in sixth grade, I was always on the phone. One day I was talking to a schoolmate named Clarence. We had been talking on the phone for about an hour and a half. My brother picked up the house phone and told me he wanted to use it. I would have let him, but he said it rudely. So I kept talking to Clarence. About twenty minutes later I heard the phone pick up. Clarence didn't. He just kept talking and said he wanted to "do it to me." All I heard was "Oh *hell* no, baby girl!" followed by a whole bunch of curse words I never even knew went together in a sentence.

My parents were better than any detective I've ever seen. Within an hour, my parents had Clarence's address and phone number. By seven o'clock that evening, I was sitting in Clarence's living room with his parents. I was so embarrassed. My parents made sure that this boy never came near me again. When we got home that night, I thought I would never see the light of day again. But I received a short punishment for what happened.

That night my mom and I had a talk. She talked about me respecting myself and my body. Respecting myself meant never allowing anyone(especially a boy) to put me down, degrade me, or tell me that I could not accomplish my dreams. Respect included what I allowed boys to say or do to me.

My mom told me that a female's body is very precious. Every girl must cleanse it, love it, and, most of all, guard it. She went on to explain that there will be boys who would deceive me with nice words and promise to give me things in order to take advantage of me. And to never allow myself to be swindled out of my innocence.

My mom used the story of how she and my dad met to get me to understand better: My dad and his brothers had a reputation for being the "bad boys" around town. They were mischievous and were into everything. But when he met my mom, he did what he had to do to let her know she was special. It was more than words. He walked her to school and spent time with her family, and his words were always kind. He earned her respect and the respect of her family. If he ever had ulterior motives, he never let them be known because he knew if he wasn't true to my mom, that would be the deal breaker and he would never have a chance to be with her.

My mom ended her talk by letting me know that she and my dad loved me very much, and if any boy really liked me, he would never talk to me like that. Finally, if I ever needed anything, they would always be there for me.

Ray, My New Friend

Ray and I spent the last few weeks before school laughing and getting to know each other. After I got over what she appeared to be, I realized we had a lot in common. Both of us played basketball and loved R&B, pop, and hip-hop music. She was an honor student and was going to St. Augustine's on a scholarship too. I also found out that she had a stepdad. Her parents never married but parted ways when she was just a few months old. She hadn't even known who her dad was until a few years ago. Although she heard many bad things about her father cheating on her mother, she loved the fact that he was back in her life.

And then there were the twins. She admitted the twins were cute when they were younger, but now they were "double terrors." She loved them but tried her best to separate herself from them.

We even started to think about what activities we wanted to do this school year. Ray was nothing like I expected. Throughout the weeks, she invited me over for dinner a few times, but I had to pass. I was still on medication and most of the time I just wanted to go to sleep. Plus the thought of being at the dinner table with those crazy twins made me appreciate the craziness within my own family.

Right before she left my house one night, she let me know that Tommy had asked about me. I started blushing and smiling. I couldn't hide that I liked him. "I'll take that as, tell him you said hi," she said, giggling as she left the room. I lay in my bed thinking about Tommy all night long.

Two Days until School

I was excited as school approached. With only a couple of days left, my mom took me, Ray, and Ray's mom to the local mall.

Every store was having a back-to-school sale. We stood in front of the Macy's and set a time when we would meet our moms. Once our watches were synchronized, we went off into the mall.

I had gone to the uniform store the day before, so all I needed to find were shoes and accessories. My parents always took me shoe shopping, but this year was too important to leave it in their hands. I was going to high school, and there was no way that I was going to walk into a new school with a pair of orthopedic grandma-looking shoes (even if I only had one good foot). I found the cutest pair of shoes in one of my favorite stores, and they were on sale! So, I bought two pairs.

Ray and I left the shoe store. We decided to take a break after two hours of shoe shopping and go to the food court. My mom and Ray's mom were taking a break as well. They waved us over. I needed to sit. My arms were tired from walking around with crutches all day. We showed our moms the great deals we got on shoes, earrings, book bags, and the other things we just had to have.

All of a sudden, I heard some guys talking. It was Damian pointing to me and telling a group of boys about my pothole accident. They laughed. I felt my face turning warm with anger. *Jerk!* I thought. "Not all of us are like that."

When I turned around, Tommy was standing right behind me. "Don't mind him," he said. All I could do was smile and nod. He looked around the table and greeted everyone and reintroduced himself to my mom. She thanked him again for bringing me home after my fall. He turned to me and said, "I heard you can play some ball." I turned to Ray and gave her the eye as if I was going to kill her. *They have been talking behind my back. What have they been saying?*

"I play a little."

"Well I expect a game when you're healed. I'll take it easy on you."

"Whatever," I replied. "Don't hold back. Bring it." We both smiled, and he returned to his friends. My mom saw me as I watched him leave. She started giggling.

About two hours later, we returned home from a long day of shopping. I was exhausted. Once again I lay across my bed. I was ready for school. It was comforting to know that Ray was going to St. Augustine's too. And of course, that Tommy was at St. Andrews.

Chapter 2
1st Quarter

The First Day of School

I looked perfect. The scars on my face had healed. The swelling was gone from my leg. My blue cast matched perfectly with my uniform, which was neatly pressed and fell to a few inches above my knee. It was short enough to "fit in" and long enough so I wouldn't look like a "ho." The last thing I needed was to develop that type of reputation on the first day of school.

I went to my stylist the day before, so my hair was easy to do. I just unwrapped my scarf and made sure the sides were neatly lying down. I admired myself in the mirror: *Hey, Beautiful! You will have the best day of school and the best school year. You will be on the honor roll. You will make new friends, and the boys will love you!*

I blew myself a kiss and smiled. That made me giggle, but I left the house filled with confidence. My days of being teased about being a tomboy were gone. This was the start of a new school year. This was a new beginning.

In the mornings, I carpooled with Ray and her dad. In the afternoons, my dad would give me a ride home until my cast was removed. The deal was after my cast was removed, I had to ride the metro bus. Ray had piano lessons and her club meetings after school, so she stayed after for three hours every day.

Ray was kind of a geek, but when I got to know her, she was actually a really cool … geek. Her parents, like mine, wanted her to be something in life. But the difference was, her mother lived her dreams vicariously through Ray. She had Ray in all kinds of activities—music lessons, science club, engineering club, and Girl Scouts. I understood that her mother wanted her to be successful in life, but dang, Ray needed to have fun too! Although Ray rarely got a break, when she got a chance to relax, she knew how to have fun.

We were both excited. We talked the whole way to school trying to figure out how high school would be different from middle school. We hoped there wouldn't be too many differences. It took me all of elementary and most of middle school to make a name for myself. My classmates finally came around from their warped sense of thinking during my eighth grade year. I was the cool, down-to-earth athlete and honor roll student that everyone wanted to be friends with instead of the awkward, geeky, thick tomboy that I used to be.

When I lived at my grandma's, the kids in her neighborhood acted like it was cool for kids to be stupid and to be in trouble. You often saw kids hanging on the corners all day long. And I never saw anyone carrying a book bag that was actually filled with books! Apparently they did not have parents like mine in their homes.

My brother almost fell into that trap. He was hanging with the wrong people on the street. In school, he would hide his books and homework from his friends because none of them were doing well in school. He stayed in the streets with his boys until the wee hours of the night doing little hustling jobs and would wake up early to do his homework. My parents ended up giving him a curfew to keep him from coming in so late. When he was late, my brother would claim that his small-time hustles were helping the family pay the bills, since my dad was struggling to find a steady job.

Thank goodness my father was a strong man. As soon as those words came out my brother's mouth, my dad would cut him off and let him know how the world really worked and how society portrayed young African American men. My father talked about his personal struggles and the struggles of his family, which enabled him to get to where he was. Every once in a while, my brother would snap back at him by saying things like "I'm not gonna be like you. I'm always gonna be able to take care of my family."

My father just nodded and replied, "All my struggles for my family have been worth it. And through it all I have taken care of you. Everyone will struggle. There is no such thing as a perfect life. Even celebrities have issues. Money does not make life easy or better. When people try to take shortcuts in life, like that hustling thing you're doing in the streets, there may be instant gratification but not a long-term sense of pride or accomplishment."

My mother didn't talk a lot, she just did what she had to do. She showed us that education was important. She showed us that we needed sacrifice and hard work to get ahead. I learned a lot from watching my family interact. I used to get mad about how I always had to study hard, visit museums, go to plays, and even participate in family nights. But now when I see the ignorance of other kids, I understand why they raised me the way they did.

My New School

The staff and administration moved all the students into the auditorium. Last year, our middle school had a place called the multipurpose room. It was our cafeteria, gym, and auditorium bundled into one room. This place, on the other hand, was huge! All of the freshmen were placed in the first fifteen rows of the auditorium. The teachers were all sitting on stage according to their subjects, and then the headmaster strutted out on stage. Students began to stand up, burst out in screams and whistles, and cheer. You could tell that the students loved the headmaster. After a five minute standing ovation, he motioned for everyone to get quiet. When the room was silent, he began with a prayer.

After the prayer, the next twenty minutes or so were spent on explaining opening day procedures, introducing the teachers, and talking about his expectations for the school year. He wanted every girl to be successful and encouraged us to look our best, act our best, and be our best. He reminded us that we were chosen to be here and to continue being the great ladies we came here to be. He ended with a quote from the late Nelson Mandela: "Education is the most powerful weapon for you to change the world." And then he charged us to "go out and change the world."

Those simple words made me feel inspired. I got the feeling that everyone here wanted me to succeed. At that very moment, I didn't quite know what I was going to do or be in my future, but I promised myself that I would try my best and always be the best me I could be.

Ray and I stood next to each other in the line to pick up our schedules. We knew we would not be in any classes together. Ray had decided that she would go the Science and Technology track. She had researched the need for engineers, and being a biracial female was just a bonus for college scholarships. I, on the other hand, had no clue as to what I wanted to do. Being grown up and having a career seemed far down the road. I just never took the time to think about it.

I looked at my schedule. I had freshman English, Biology, Algebra I, French, Physical Education, American History, Religion, and Technology. I thought my head was going to explode just looking at all the classes I was taking. But what I had was nothing compared to Ray's Algebra II, Physics, and Introduction to Engineering classes. Our classes were at opposite ends of the school, so our lockers were on different floors. Although it felt like we were being cruelly torn apart, we knew that we would see each other at lunch.

I took a deep breath and put my notebooks in the locker. I didn't have time to decorate the inside with the items I'd bought at the mall. I figured I could make time for that tomorrow. I was off to my first class. The school was not as big as I initially thought, yet I felt like a salmon swimming against the current—in this case a river of girls. Without Ray by my side, I already felt small and alone.

When I'd left home this morning, I thought I looked cute and felt confident. I knew I would easily fit in. But compared to these girls, I looked like I was still in elementary school and just cute. These girls looked like grown women. They were beautiful. They had hips, thighs—even breasts like a grown woman. There were big girls, skinny girls, light-skinned and dark-skinned girls. I even saw a few pregnant girls among the masses. Not that I had never seen a pregnant person but they had always been older or at least out of high school.

I finally made it to my first class, freshman English, after being pushed around trying to make my way to class. It was nice to be among people who also looked overwhelmed by our new lives. Sister Mary Francis came to the front of the room and introduced herself. She was soft spoken and well mannered. I knew I had this class in the bag … until she gave us the syllabus for the year. I had twenty novels to read including *To Kill a Mockingbird, Chinese*

Cinderella: A Story of an Unwanted Daughter, and *I Know Why the Caged Bird Sings*. And of course reading twenty books meant writing twenty papers.

We had a vocabulary test every week, grammar assignments, oral presentations and a group project. My head was throbbing just reading the list of assignments I had to do. Sister Mary Francis could tell by our faces that we were in a state of shock from the assignments given. All she could say was "Welcome to high school, ladies," and smiled. I think she actually received some kind of strange pleasure from the pain we were all feeling.

By lunchtime I was very glad to find Ray. I couldn't believe the nerve of these teachers giving me all this work. I even had papers to write for Physical Education. Who writes papers in PE? Aren't you supposed to play games in PE? Whatever happened to doing the presidential fitness test or playing team sports? Man, I had an entirely different mental picture of what high school was going to be like. Not only were my classes different, so were the girls—I mean the women.

"How will I ever get to know the boys of St. Andrews if I have to compete against these women and spend my life inside the house completing all this schoolwork?" Ray laughed at me. She thought my babbling was silly. She told me to focus on my work, and all that other stuff (like boys and popularity) would come later.

That was easy for her to say. Her high-functioning, anal-retentive brain automatically sucked up the English language and mathematical problems like a sponge and spit out answers to equations like a well-trained dog. On the other hand, I had to work five times as hard for my grades. By the end of lunch, I had already mentally prepared myself for my afternoon classes. Nothing my afternoon teachers could tell me would surprise me like my morning teachers had.

I finally got through the first day of school. I had to wait for my dad to pick me up because he wouldn't let me ride the bus on crutches. While I sat on the front steps of the school, a group of upperclassmen walked by, and one could obviously tell they were close friends. They giggled like they were gossiping. After zoning in on their conversation, I was able to hear that they were cheerleaders for St. Andrews. They were planning on hanging out with the varsity football players this weekend.

They must have sensed I was eavesdropping. They stared at me like I had some type of disease. They were silent for a minute, rolled their eyes, tossed their fake cheerleader ponytails over their shoulders, turned their backs to me, and continued their conversation.

My dad pulled up. He got out of the car, grabbed my book bag, and helped me get in the car. I loved my daddy. He was such a gentleman. He would always remind me that the way he treated me was what I should always seek and demand from any guy. (He also never forgot to add that I couldn't date until I was twenty-five.) As we were going home, he asked me lots of questions about my first day of school. I tried to act like I was as excited as he was, but I still needed a moment to take in all of today's events.

I went right into the house and hobbled up to my room. I immediately turned on my computer. My parents didn't allow me to have a TV or telephone in my room. I begged, pleaded, took on new chores—the whole nine yards. It was a battle I tried to win many, many times. But once again the *"old school"* way of life prevailed. What they didn't realize was that all the TV programs I missed, I could see on my desktop. So they thought they had won this fight, but I was still a small step ahead.

I sat in my window. Once again I began to stare aimlessly into the sky. I replayed all the events of the day in my mind. I thought about how much older the upperclassman looked. I thought about all the schoolwork I was given. I thought about—

In the middle of my daydreaming my eyes came into focus, and I saw Tommy leaving Ray's house. They were laughing and conversing. They gave each other a hug. Suddenly Tommy looked up and waved. *Oh my God. He can see me. I feel like a stalker.*

I smiled and waved back. *What were they laughing about? How long was he at her house?* Why *was he at her house?* I felt my face start to warm up. Was I getting mad or jealous? How could I? He didn't even see me like that. In that moment I snapped back into reality. He was an athlete. He probably only liked the popular cheerleader type, and that was not me.

I tried to get thoughts of Tommy out of my mind. Finally, I was able to focus on my homework. Here was something I never understood. What was the purpose of classes like Algebra or Biology? I didn't plan on ever using it in life. I didn't plan on being an engineer, and for sure I didn't see me cutting somebody open for surgery. Even though the purpose of these classes was unclear, I did understand that my parents were not accepting any grades lower than a B. So whether it was my future plan to use these subjects or not, I had to do well in all my classes.

Friday morning I went to my doctor's appointment. My leg was totally healed, and my cast was removed. It had been a grueling month and a half. I was thankful that I no longer had to haul a heavy leg around or have those crutches chafe my armpits. On Saturday morning, I even had the nerve to go for a bike ride-that was the reason why I was in the stupid cast. It felt like forever since I'd been able to ride. I rode all through the neighborhood. I was glad I went riding because facing that fear made me feel free.

On my way back to the house, I saw Tommy practicing in his driveway. I pulled up, and he started laughing. "Well, if it isn't lil' hopalong."

"Oh, you got jokes. They're just as bad as your basketball skills!"

"Oh, you think you can handle my ball better than me?" he said as he propped it right in front of him like he was grabbing his private parts.

"Whatever. I got this." I stole the ball and did a perfect layup. He looked surprised and realized, I am not just talking junk, I can really play! He checked the ball again. This time, he was dazed and confused as my crossover left him standing in the same place as I coasted to the basket. "What? I can't hear you! Can't wait to tell your friends you got beat by a girl?" He looked like he was getting upset. I looked in his face. "Oh, I see you like to be the teaser but not the one being teased."

He grabbed the ball from my hand and said, "Girl, I was just playing with you. Let Big Daddy show you how it's done." He got around me once and made it to the hole. After that, it was on! We played a vicious game of one-on-one. He was so close to me when he was playing defense, I could barely move. I tried to stick my butt out to push him back. He caught on to my strategy, so he moved in closer. I could feel him on me. I could feel *all* of him. Then I was distracted.

He won by one point. He did say he was surprised at how well I kept up. He usually beats the mess out of his friends. "Well, I think you need to practice more. You know I just got out of my cast today. Next time I will not be so nice," I said, smoothing my shirt over my sweatpants.

My leg was throbbing, but I acted like I felt no pain at all. I'd done way too much. I went to get my bike, and he scooted past me to pick it up. He looked me right in the face, and his hazel eyes left me feeling like melted butter on a pancake. He put his hand on top of mine while I straddled my bike. "Thanks for the game," I said. It looked like he was going to kiss me. I leaned forward like

I was catching my pedal but I really wanted a kiss. He just looked at me. He didn't even try. Embarrassed by rejection, I decided to ride off. He watched me as I turned the corner. I rushed home to take my medication, take a shower, and change my clothes.

Ray and I decided to celebrate my cast removal by taking a trip to the mall and later to the movies. When we got to the mall, we walked around to our favorite stores and decided to grab a bite to eat before the movies. We sat at the food court. I bought my usual chicken quesadilla from the Taco Bell with a milkshake from Dairy Queen. I was in heaven.

After several minutes of silence, I told Ray about the morning at Tommy's house. I even told her about our kissable moment. Ray looked at me like I was crazy. We were engaged in deep conversation when all of a sudden, we could hear high-pitched giggling behind us. It was the group of cheerleaders I'd seen many times after school. They were beautiful and bubbly, and the jocks loved them. They dressed in tight clothes and wore lots of makeup. Part of me wanted to look like those size-two looking baby dolls. But with my physical proportions and athleticism, I knew it was not possible.

I couldn't believe what I saw or should I say *who* I saw in the middle of the group. *Tommy*. I knew that he liked the cheerleader type. I stared him down really hard, hoping he could feel my eyes on him. But it did not faze him. He was having the time of his life. He had the captain of the junior varsity cheerleader sitting on his lap. They were laughing. She was feeding him his lunch and wiping his mouth. She whispered in his ear. He saw me looking at him. I could feel my face getting warm. I wanted to smack the crap out of him, but instead I just stared.

He raised his eyebrows, smiled, and gave me a nod. Then he rubbed one hand along her thigh. She squirmed, and it wasn't with disapproval. She moved against his hand. They started kissing. You could see her ramming her tongue down his throat. *They should be embarrassed all out in public like that. Why don't they get a room?* It was like the other cheerleaders, his boys, and the rest of the shoppers in the food court were not even there. In my eyes, Tommy went from sexy to gross in 5 seconds. But part of me still wanted a part of him.

"He doesn't even know we're here," Ray said. "Let's face it: we're a whole different breed of girl." I thought about it, and Ray was right. I was surprised she would say something like that. How quickly she could forget about the day I saw him leaving her house. I know he saw me. I still thought I had a small chance to win him over. I thought we'd had a moment at his house—a connection.

I looked down at myself. Today, I looked like my typical self- just like a boy. I had on a pair of jeans, our local basketball team jersey, and my favorite pair of sneakers. My hair was pulled back in a ponytail. *How can I compete with the captain of the cheerleaders? I never wanted to; I don't plan on it. There is nothing wrong with what I am wearing. I'm comfortable. I'm me!*

We went to see the movie that had just opened the night before. We'd had to get our tickets as soon as we got to the mall because the show was bound to be sold out. I tried to focus on the movie. It might have actually been funny, but I was distracted by the memory of Tommy and that girl. I thought when I moved to the county, there was a chance things would be different but today was just another example of me being invisible to boys.

My First Crush

After I had switched to the room with my brother at my grandparents' house, our relationship began to change. I hung out with him more. We were close. His sports team was my sports team; his friends were my friends, until I got a crush on his friend Chuck.

Chuck was a few years older than me. He was fine, light-skinned with a toned body, curly hair, and big puppy-dog brown eyes. A perfect description would be a man with the body of a God. I thought Chuck and I would be great together. We loved the same basketball team, loved the same music, and shared the same friends. I thought we had enjoyable conversations. He always told me how cute I was.

One day I saw him at the basketball court with my cousin Angie. She knew I liked him, but she didn't care. She saw me and began to kiss him. As they were holding each other, he reached down and grabbed her butt. She looked uncomfortable but tried to fake being unflustered because she knew I was looking. He whispered in her ear; she giggled. He grabbed her hand, and they walked down the street to his house. I couldn't believe what she had done behind my back (well, actually, in front of my face).

Later that day my brother, his friends, and I met up at Chuck's house, which they called "the clubhouse." They were trying to make plans to celebrate Chuck's birthday. Chuck didn't care about any of the activities. He was just concerned about what girls he wanted to invite to the party. Come to find out that Angie meant nothing to him. My feelings were torn. On the one hand, I felt good because Angie deserved everything she got. On the other hand, Chuck was showing his true colors. He was a dog.

That Saturday, Chuck had his party. Every kid on the block was trying to get in. I watched Chuck from afar. The entire night Chuck was surrounded by girls. He smiled at some. He kissed others. Even though he did what he did with Angie and was kissing on these other girls, I still liked him. I approached him. I tried to make conversation about last night's basketball game. He was looking around me as if I wasn't even there. He asked me to bring him a drink. As I stepped away toward the drink table, he grabbed another girl's hand and pulled her close. I watched him fondle her chest and whisper in her ear, and once again he headed into the house with another one of his conquests. He didn't care about any of those girls. He just wanted to "hook up." He didn't even notice me. He actually treated me like I was my brother's kid sister—or worse, like I was just one of the boys. I hated being invisible ….

Let It Go, Girl!

I went to bed a little sad that night. It wasn't like Tommy was my boyfriend (Daddy wouldn't have that), but I just thought that he could be a different type of friend. Monday, back at school, I was focused on my schoolwork. It felt good to be walking around and not struggling with all my work plus a set of crutches.

I walked into the cafeteria and sat with the usual crew. Everyone was smiling as they passed around a piece of paper. It was a flyer announcing how to run for homecoming queen and princess. St. Andrew's was having their homecoming dance. I was excited. I had never been to a high school dance before. I flashed back to what had happened with Tommy at the mall last weekend and immediately convinced myself that I should not go because there was no chance in hell I would get a date. It would be so embarrassing. I refused to allow my first impression to others, to show that I am a lonely person. I snapped back into reality when the bell for my next class rang. I got up quickly and headed off to class. Ray called for me, but I didn't look back. I got there early for religion class, but it didn't matter. I needed time to think. No, I needed time to pray.

Dear God,

Help me. Why can't I be more like the cheerleaders?
They're so perfect. Perfect looks, perfect boyfriends …
When is it going to be my chance to shine?
When will people notice me?
Help me, Lord. Help me.
Amen.

Time felt like it was taking its sweet ol' time, and I was ready for the day to be over. Finally the last bell rang. Since I was off my crutches, my parents wanted me to start taking the bus home. We lived in the county, so it took me a bus, the subway, and another bus to get home. Altogether, it was about two hours until I felt the comfort of my bed.

After a few minutes of relaxing, I completed my homework and went downstairs to eat dinner. My dad was working late on a project, so it was just me and my mom. She asked me about my day. I told her about the homecoming announcement, and that I didn't want to go. I told her that I didn't think I would ever get a date. She asked me if there was anyone I was interested in. That was my cue to give her a parent-suitable version of what had happened with Tommy on Saturday.

She asked me why I wanted to be the girl sitting on Tommy's lap. *What kind of question is that? This woman has got things twisted.* I told her it wasn't like that. I told her I thought he was cute, but I couldn't go to the dance because I didn't think anyone would want to dance with me, and I wasn't about to lean against the wall with the nerds all night.

I was getting upset and ready to walk away when my mom gave me a big hug and explained to me that not every girl develops the same way and at the same time. "Keep focusing on your schoolwork, and all the other things in life will fall into place."

She sounded like Ray. I wondered if they had been talking. I went back to my room, still upset from our conversation. I understood what my mother was saying, but it was not what I wanted to hear.

The next day at school, the hallways were transformed. Several girls had put up posters and were wearing buttons reminding people to vote for the homecoming court. Right before I walked in the cafeteria, I heard a familiar voice say, "Vote for me." It was the slutty cheerleader who'd been sitting on Tommy's lap. She smiled and handed me a button. *I know she really doesn't expect me to vote for her. She doesn't even know who I am.* To her, I was just another freshman, another vote. To me, she was just the slut who'd stolen my future husband. Even though technically she had him first.

Weeks went by, and the battle for homecoming was getting malicious. You would think that being at a Catholic school would make a difference, that everyone walks around with rosy cheeks and prayerful hands. Think again. That theory, for me, flew out the window on day one when I counted five pregnant girls, noticed a girl smoking weed while hanging out the bathroom window, heard students cussing out their teachers, and the list goes on.

These perfect examples of "church" girls were ripping down posters, creating smear campaigns (talking about who slept with whom to get in the campaign race), and even started several fights after school. It was getting so out of control that the headmaster had to call an "all school" assembly.

He started with a prayer (as always) and went right into his sermon. He discussed how certain behaviors will never be tolerated by young ladies. How would this school create young female leaders of tomorrow if we could not show common decency and have good sportsmanship? His speech lasted for about thirty-five minutes, and then we were dismissed to our last period class. As soon as we were outside in the hallway, not even seven minutes after the headmaster spoke, I heard Ms. Slut say she still planned on winning. What frightened me was the threat "by any means necessary."

I couldn't believe what I heard. The girl was clueless. She had distorted the meaning of some of the most powerful words spoken by Malcolm X, one of our most influential African American leaders. That statement was used when blacks were subjected to having few or no rights, living in conditions that were unbearable, and being considered less than human. The country was at war, and Malcolm had to fight "by any means necessary." He was fighting for people to get a good education, the right to vote, and the right to walk with their heads held high and not to be belittled or degraded as human beings. She just wanted to win a stupid little homecoming event. She didn't care. Most people our age don't care. Young ignorance wins again! Some of these girls were ridiculous. I couldn't believe I'd thought she was better than me. I just shook my head and went to class.

When the last bell of the day rang, I took my two-hour daily journey home. I needed to release my frustration, so I dragged my portable basketball court out of the garage. I hadn't played or practiced since that day with Tommy. I thought I would be playing this season, but I was still rehabilitating my injured ankle. I played for about forty-five minutes and then went into the house to shower, eat, and do my homework.

Once again it was just me and my mom at the dinner table. She asked me the usual questions about my day. And then she asked me if I was going to homecoming. I told her that I still did not want to go.

The Friday before homecoming week, the homecoming committee announced all the winners. The captain of the varsity cheerleaders was named queen, and the junior varsity team captain, the one I couldn't stand, Tommy's plaything, won for the sophomore princess.

Homecoming week was fun. Even though it was actually St. Andrew's who was having the game, we got a chance to participate in all of the activities. I was so excited because we got a chance to be out of uniform for the entire week. Every day of the week had a different theme. Pajama day was on Monday. I wore a cute pair of pajama pants and a T-shirt. Being out of uniform made me too comfortable; I didn't even feel like doing any type of schoolwork.

And of course, there were some girls that took pajama day to a whole nother level—a Victoria's Secret level. I don't know who they were looking cute for in an all girls' school, but I guess they thought that someone would like it. Those girls were sent home immediately. The headmaster got on the intercom right before I went to lunch. He told us if we could not handle ourselves properly, including our dress, he would cancel this week for us.

Fortunately, everyone else was willing to adhere to his request. The teachers even joined in the festivities! They had to be more lenient about classwork because they knew our attention spans were really short. On some days they even dressed up like the students.

We had a good time the rest of the week. Twin day was lots of fun. Ray and I decided to dress alike. We wore our matching Adidas sweat suits. Ray's mom picked them up for us from New York when she went on a business trip. We could tell people were jealous. They asked us where we got them and told us how cute we looked, but you could tell by their faces that they were just hatin'. I loved it!

The next day was school spirit day- which we had pep rally

and wore our school colors. For class spirit day we had individual colors for each class and competed in several competitions to see who had the best class.

That night, I went home and did my regular routine. I played basketball for about forty minutes and ran to my room to take a shower. When I walked in, I saw the most beautiful dress on my bed. It was hot pink, with a long slit up the side. I held it up against me in front of the mirror. As I whirled around, my parents were standing in the doorway. They startled me. My mom was smiling, and my dad had that concerned but happy look on his face. They wanted me to go to the school's first dance. I couldn't say no, plus I was having so much fun all week, I wanted to go.

Friday was jersey day. Everyone wore a different basketball or football jersey to support their favorite team. We also played basketball and even had a powder-puff football game. The boys of St. Andrews were invited to the football game. I don't know if the guys were more excited to get out of class or to see all the girls tackling each other on the field. No matter, we all had a good time. Ray and I found Tommy and his crew and sat with them. They were impressed by my throwback jersey of Ray Lewis when he played for the University of Miami. I didn't say much. I just smiled. We danced, shouted chants, and had a good time. At the end of the game, our entire school did a cheer to show our support for St. Andrews and their big game on Saturday.

My parents—well, really my mom—had set up a morning of pampering on Saturday. It was like a rite of passage from a boyish little girl to a beautiful young lady. My mom went to the salon with me. We got our hair done, manicures, and pedicures. When I left the salon, I felt like a princess and looked like an entirely different girl—or like my mom says, a proper young lady (with a horrible British accent).

The whole evening was set up with the help of Ray's parents.

When I came down the steps, my mom was crying like she was giving me away at my wedding. My dad was acting like he was a professional photographer and I was on *America's Next Top Model*. Ray was waiting at the bottom of the stairs with her family. My dad gave me a wrist corsage. Once again, he reminded me that this is the kind of treatment I should expect from a young man; anything less was unacceptable.

Ray's parents drove us to the dance, and my parents were designated to pick us up. We stepped into the gym of St. Andrew's. It had been transformed into a beautiful castle fit for royalty. I hoped I was making some kind of grand entrance, but really no one noticed when I walked in. I was very nervous. Ray immediately found some people from her engineering club. I encouraged her to go talk to them. I didn't want her to feel like she was stuck babysitting me. I slowly wandered around the outskirts of the gym. I refused to end up sitting along the wall with the nerds, the ugly and most pitiful, the lonely.

I couldn't believe how many people were there. Everyone was talking about the game earlier and how St. Andrew's dominated St. Francis. I missed the game. I was at the salon getting pampered.

"I was looking for you at the game, Tumbles."

"Excuse me," I replied and turned around. It was Damian, Tommy's best friend. "Oh, you're not funny. And as you can see, I'm all healed." I lifted my dress up a little and poked my leg out through the slit. I tightened my calf to show him my firm muscles. I stepped back and gave a model-type twirl to show off my newfound image.

"Yes, I can see you have healed ... and nicely, too." He raised his eyebrows, trying to hide his nervousness. "So now that you have those new legs, you ready to show me what you do with them?"

"Excuse me?"

"I mean—Mademoiselle, may I have this dance?" he asked, bowing like a prince to a princess. I wanted to say no to him because of how cruel he'd been to me at the mall. But tonight he seemed a little different. He looked hopeless, kinda like a sad puppy. I couldn't resist.

So with a cute little curtsey I smiled and said, "Hell no, but thank you," and started to walk away. Then he grabbed my hand firmly and led me into the crowd. We danced about six or seven songs. I couldn't believe what a good dancer he was.

Then it happened. He pulled me close and I could hear my favorite R&B singer singing to me. We were slow dancing—cheek to cheek, chest to chest, and pelvis to …. *Oh my God. Is that what I think it is?* I felt him move and grow. *I wonder what it feels like. What does it look like?* My body tingled. My mind started to wander. *I never thought about Damian like this. Is this, like, cheating on Tommy? I'm tripping.*

All of a sudden he looked at his watch, excused himself, and rushed off. He said he would be back in a little bit and asked me not to leave. I said okay and walked back over to the bleachers on the side. I couldn't believe he'd left me. I looked at the clock on the wall. He was gone almost a half hour. I felt something I already knew too well: *rejection.*

I don't know what I was doing trusting a fool like him. I mean, he's friends with the other fool, Tommy. I know we live in two different social worlds. People like him don't come around people like me unless it's to embarrass us or make him look good by helping the "less fortunate."

I'd seen all the movies, read all the stories, and, most of all, had enough experiences to know the outcome. I walked to the bathroom. And Ray was inside. She was excited and said she was having the time of her life. I was happy for her. She asked me about my time and could sense that all was not well. "Okay, what did that Tommy boy do now?"

"Actually it's not him," I replied. "It's no big deal." I fixed my dress and my hair and left the bathroom.

I walked back into the gym. The football coach was on stage giving a heartfelt speech about his awesome team. He praised them for the effort that they had shown all season. Then he introduced the homecoming court. Everyone started cheering. I really didn't care who won. Everyone knew these contests were rigged. Only the girls who "put out" the most got crowned the queen and princesses. And the guys who got all the girls were named the king and princes.

The coach introduced the freshman prince and princess. Then there was Tommy and his permanently attached cheerleader. Next came the junior prince, *Damian*, with his cheerleader. Last of all, the king and queen were the varsity football and cheerleading captains. It took me a moment to digest. Damian was a prince, but why was he dancing with me?

After the introduction of the homecoming court, the couples danced together. I had watched long enough. I should have known better. I felt like I didn't belong.

I started walking toward the door when I heard someone yell, "Tumbles, where are you going?" I lied and said I just needed some air when in actuality I wanted to hide my tears, go outside, and wait in the cold for two hours for my parents to pick me up. "Girl, come back here and dance with me!"

I smiled and once again couldn't resist those eyes and his smile. He held my hand firmly and, for the second time tonight, took me to the middle of the floor. All of a sudden, "The Wobble" started playing. All the girls started lining up to do the line dance. "I'm going to show you how we do it back home," Damian whispered in my ear. He stepped back, did a little "Usher" twirl and started to dance. He was doing the Wobble but added his own flavor. He was turning and moving with the group but he was so smoove with his moves.

Back in the Day

Before we moved to my grandparents' house, my parents threw many basement parties. There would be about two dozen people eating, drinking, and grooving to Marvin Gaye, Stevie Wonder, and Chuck Brown. They would party all night long.

On several occasions, my daddy caught me peeking down the steps. He would call out my name, bring me downstairs, and teach me dance moves. My mom would always cut in. She was the better dancer. But because of them, I knew how to step and groove with the best.

Shake It Fast … Show Them What I'm Working With

Damian and I danced so well together that others began to notice. The next thing you know, we were in the middle of the dance floor, and everyone was watching us. I got nervous. He could feel my body starting to back away. "Don't leave me now, Tumbles." He pulled me closer and gave me that smile again.

Finally the song ended. For a brief moment, I was the center of attention. I was a freshman dancing with the junior homecoming prince. And within minutes I was back to "Who are you again?" status.

I had to admit I'd had a lot of fun. On my way home, I couldn't stop talking. I thanked my parents for all that they did for me. If it wasn't for them, I would have missed out on the best night ever. Ray told them all about my dancing moment with

Damian. My parents were proud that I took a chance, and so was I.

I had to admit that the moment with Damian boosted my popularity. There were upperclassmen who talked to me in the hallways, and then there were the cheerleaders who hated on me because I danced with one of "their" men. All I could say was that he chose me.

Overall, my first quarter of high school was pretty good. My GPA was a 3.3, I got my cast off, and I went to my first high school dance. Unfortunately, I didn't see or talk to Damian after the dance. I didn't know if that was what he wanted or just the way things were. But either way I couldn't wait for what was next: my birthday.

Chapter 3
2nd Quarter

DE-DELICIOUS: Hey, girl, W's goin on?

SUNSHYNE: Just working on my Physics project. We are entering this competition for NSBE.

DE-DELICIOUS: NSBE?

SUNSHYNE: Yeah, the National Society of Black Engineers.

DE- DELICIOUS: Dang, girl, you are on it!

SUNSHYNE: Gotta be. I'm trying to make things happen!

DE-DELICIOUS: That's what I'm talkin about! Do the damn thing!

SUNSHINE: LOL

DE-DELICIOUS: So, I've been trying to decide what to do for my birthday.

SUNSHYNE: Are you having a party?

DE-DELICIOUS: Nahhh. My daddy still thinks that a clown is appropriate for his baby girl. I was thinking we could go somewhere.

SUNSHYNE: Like where? Who will you invite?

DE-DELICIOUS: I have no idea.

All of a sudden, in the middle of my chat another instant message appeared.

DrDetroit: Ws up?

DeDelicious: Who is this?

DrDetroit: Oh you don't know who I am now?

DeDelicious: Didn't I ask you who you are?

DrDetroit: Feisty … I like that in my woman.

DeDelicious: Your woman? Who the hell is this?

DrDetroit: You not even going to guess? Dang, why are you makin it hard for a brotha?

DeDelicious: No, a brotha made it hard for himself when he didn't call, visit, or even send up a smoke signal after the dance.

DrDetroit: oooooo, So you do know who I am.

DeDelicious: Yeah, and you must take me for one of those fake dumb cheerleader broads that you mess with. How did you get my ID?

DrDetroit: Why does it have to be like that? What did they ever do to you? I wanted to talk to you. I thought we had somethin else. Maybe even somethin special. I guess I was wrong. I'm out.

If he only knew. Although I got through the first part of the school semester pretty easily as far as academics, those cheerleaders had a way of making me feel like I was below them. I think I even would have been okay if I had joined the basketball team. At least some people would have my back besides Ray. From the cheerleaders' physical attributes to their popularity, I couldn't compete.

I went to bed feeling even more insecure than before. Why should I feel bad? For the last three weeks, Damian had been the one acting like I didn't exist. *I don't understand why he's questioning me like this. Why did he come looking for me? Did he expect me to be excited to hear from him? What did those girls say about me when he danced with me all night and not them? Why was he taking up for those crazy cheerleaders? What does or shall I say did he want from me? Did I mess things up?*

I spent about three hours convincing myself that I'd done nothing wrong before I finally drifted off to sleep.

The next few weeks were rough. I felt like everyone was being mean to me or ignoring me. Ray was caught up in her project, so we didn't hang out or talk on the phone. My mom was busy meeting with people to help start her business; there were no annoying dinner conversations. My dad was staying late to work on a huge project; there was no one to hug and take all my loneliness away. The cheerleaders at school walked by me and stared like they knew that I was talking behind their back; I didn't really care about them. And to top it all off, I hadn't heard from Damian since our conversation; I guess he didn't want to talk to me for real.

So I decided to do something about it all, starting with Damian. I started by leaving him an offline message.

DE-DELICIOUS: Damian, if you get this message, please hit me up. We need to talk.

It was a cold day in November. I stayed inside the school building for a few extra minutes, bundling myself up so that I could face the windy elements. I stepped outside and was blown back a little. After catching my balance, I began the uphill trek to my bus stop.

As I was walking, something felt strange. I looked around and nothing seemed out of the ordinary. I kept walking and picked up my pace a little. I turned around again and noticed that a car was following me. I told myself not to panic, but my heart was racing. I looked around for a place to run and saw nothing but open field. I knew I could not outrun a car. I picked up my pace even more. I could finally see the top of the hill where the other students were waiting for the bus.

The window cracked a little, and I heard someone yell "Hey, shorty." I didn't acknowledge him. "Why it gotta be like that? I'm tryin' to holla at you. Slow down, Ma!" I could see the car beginning to stop. When I saw a car door open, I ran like my life depended on it. It felt like I would never make it to the top of the hill. It was close and still so far away. My lungs were burning and I could not catch my breath. When I got to the bus stop, I blended in with the other students and watched as the car slowly drove off. I was shaking and ready to cry but I couldn't let anyone see my fear.

I was about to step on the bus when a hand grabbed my shoulder from behind. "Wait up, shorty," he said. My body started to tremble. I pushed myself forward on the bus. I twisted so that whoever was grabbing me had to let go. I found a seat near the middle of the bus. I sat on an inside seat but was still able to see out the window without anyone being able to see me. The bus finally departed and I saw Damian standing at the bus stop looking confused. As we passed the corner, I saw the car that was following me parked on the side. The guy that was calling for me, was now talking to another girl. She looked as scared as I did. I didn't recognize anyone on the bus. Usually, I knew at least one person. I had no one to talk to who could take my mind off of what had just happened. To make matters worse, I had a long ride home to think about it.

I rushed up to my room and sprawled across the bed. I cried into my pillows so that no one could hear me. I thought over and over again about what had happened. I couldn't tell my parents because they would worry me to death. I couldn't tell Ray because she had been so focused on her project and I didn't want to distract her. There was no one but me.

Bing …. I could hear the instant message come up on my computer.

DrDetroit: I thought you wanted to talk?

DeDelicious: I know but today …

DrDetroit: Today you left me hanging at the bus stop

DeDelicious: you don't understand

DrDetroit: You never gave me a chance

DeDelicious: What do you want from me?

DrDetroit: I want you to stop messin' with my head.

DeDelicious: I'm not. You have things so easy. Well, they're not as easy for me.

DrDetroit: So life's not easy. That doesn't mean you can treat people however you want.

DeDelicious: I did nothing to you

DrDetroit: That's part of the problem. I've been trying to get to know you

DeDelicious: You haven't tried shit!

DrDetroit: Well then, let me try now. What the hell was going on today?

My eyes started to well up with tears. I'm glad he could not see me. The truth was flowing through me.

<u>My Scary Truth</u>

About a month before we left my grandparents, I was hanging out with my brothers friends. We were at the "clubhouse" playing spades, and the guys were having their regular conversations about all the girls they had sex with that week, sports and video games.

The conversation about the girls was disgusting. They didn't mind telling their graphic personal experiences. These guys were having sex with girls like it was a sport or competition. They didn't care who the girls were or how they felt afterward.

I had to say something about their actions, so I asked them if they even thought of using protection, and they just laughed at me. To get an STD or, even worse, HIV meant nothing to them. It was like nothing would scare them or slow them down. So instead of going back and forth about their perverted escapades, I kindly let them know that their dicks would probably fall off in the next couple of years and that they would never be good enough for a girl like me.

Everyone stopped talking and stared at me. Chuck came up behind me, blew on my neck, and started to whisper in my ear. He told me how much I would love to feel his dick inside of me. First he would put it in my mouth and then gradually move it to other places. He told me he knew how to make a little girl like me feel like a woman. He let everyone know that he knew what I needed—what I wanted. I pulled away from him. He still had a hold on my shirt and stared like a demon in my eyes. I pushed his arm down with some force to let him know to leave me alone and left the clubhouse. I could hear all of them laughing when I left. In my mind, that was the last time I ever needed to go to the clubhouse.

The last thing I heard as I reached the last step, was Chuck saying "I want that." They are so lucky my brother did not hear the trash they were talking because he would have set him straight right then and there. I had heard that sort of thing before, but it made my body cringe to have Chuck say it to me. At one point in my life Chuck was what I wanted, but now I couldn't stand his ass. And I told him so.

A week later I was walking home from the basketball court. I had just finished playing a game of four-on-four with some neighborhood street ball legends. I felt good because my team had won. I was exhausted and just wanted a shower.

I noticed a green Caprice following me. I was turning back to look at it, and it just kept following. I walked on until I saw the first alley. I tried running because I knew all the shortcuts home.

The car sped up and headed me off at the back end of the alley, and people jumped out. I was scared. I looked at them as they drew closer and recognized them as my brother's friends. I felt relief and told them to stop playing around. They invited me to come with them back to the clubhouse to hang out with them. I told them I just wanted to go home, but they didn't want to hear that.

All of a sudden, one of them grabbed me from behind. I was able to get loose by using one of the self-defense techniques my dad had taught me. But what my dad didn't teach me was what to do if there were four people attacking me at once. I blacked out.

The next thing I knew, I was waking up on the sofa of the clubhouse. My head was hurting, and the room was spinning. There was some kind of underground rock and hip-hop remix playing in the background. I heard voices, but they sounded distant. When my vision started to come back into focus, Chuck was standing over me talking about all the things he wanted to do to me sexually. He said his feelings were hurt from the last time I was there- when I said I would never want a man like him.

I couldn't move. My body felt paralyzed. I physically could not move. I thought he was my brother's friend and therefore my friend. How could this be happening? The only thing I felt was a tear rolling down my cheek. I felt a slight draft and realized that my sweats and panties had been removed. A flurry of thoughts went through my head. I wanted to escape. But I knew that was impossible.

It was so painful. I cried and cried, but no one heard me or would help me. One guy after another took turns with me. I tried kicking, but as they took turns, someone else would hold me down. They licked me. They spit on me. They hit me. They left bruises where they grabbed me. I thought I was being tossed around like a rag doll. They laughed and coached each other on how to do it to me.

They got tired of me crying and screaming and finally took a sock and gagged me. I couldn't scream anymore. I thought I was going to choke. My body gave in. It was battered and sore. My innocence was taken away. They took me back on the street and left me in the alley where they'd grabbed me.

I was taken to the hospital and faced endless questions. I couldn't tell anyone what had happened. I knew if I did, they would come for me again. My brother was pissed. I saw the veins popping from his head. You could see in his eyes, he was going to hurt someone. I couldn't even tell him that his friends, his boys that he hung with every day, were the ones who had put me here. If he ever found out, who knew what would happen?

A couple weeks later, Chuck was found dead in that same back alley. His arms and legs were hogtied behind his back; he looked like a runaway slave, and his penis was lying beside him. His body rested there lifeless, leaving no clue of what had happened. I thought I knew. I didn't go to his funeral. If I had, I think I would have kicked the casket over, jumped on his body, and beat him until he was unrecognizable.

The day of the funeral everyone was gone but me. I went down to Angie's room. I was looking for my curling iron, which she often borrowed without asking. I started going through her bag of toiletries. I found a cloth wrapped around an object. It was a bloody knife and a Polaroid of Chuck tied up. At the bottom there was a caption. It read: "You will never do this to another girl again." Damn, Angie … Even if we didn't get along, she understood, as a girl or woman, that what he did was unacceptable.

Bing ... bing ... bing .... My computer sounded like a video game.

DrDetroit: Helllllllooo

DeDelicious: Sorry. I'm just having a hard time right now.

DrDetroit: Well if you wanna talk ..

DeDelicious: I was just bothered because I thought I was being followed today

DrDetroit: Why didn't you say something?

DeDelicious: I was scared. I just wanted to get home

DrDetroit: Damn Boo ... I'm

DeDelicious: Sorry, I know. I gotta go

I logged out quickly. I couldn't think about it anymore. I couldn't stop crying. Damian sounded sincere, but these were my issues, not his.

I was kind of distracted at school the next day. I was staring out the windows. I couldn't even focus on the words in my book. I excused myself during sixth period to go to the bathroom. I walked in and headed right into the last stall. It took everything inside of me not to break down and cry.

A few minutes later a girl entered the bathroom, talking on the phone. She was begging someone not to be mad and assuring them that "the test came out positive." She told him it was his, and no chance it could be anyone else's. She tried to talk more. Apparently, whoever was on the other end kept cutting her off. She told him she would come see him after school, but it was clear that the person on the other end had hung up.

I looked through the crack of my stall and saw it was the cheerleader: Tommy's Girl. I waited in the stall until she left the bathroom. I felt bad for her and for him. I mean, I couldn't even imagine having a baby in high school. What would they do?

I remember a girl in my seventh grade class was pregnant. My parents knew that they had to really start talking to me. What were at one time mild conversations about the birds and the bees became explicit talks (with graphics) about sex. My parents talked to me, took me to the local Planned Parenthood, and talked to me some more. What scared me the most were the consequences. I was afraid of catching diseases but even more scared of having a child before I was ready.

Finally classes were over. I was ready to go home but fearful of my walk to the bus stop. I did my daily ritual of bundling up and taking a deep breath before I stepped into the elements. Today I added an extra prayer for protection.

When I walked outside, Damian stood there smiling. He looked so handsome. I was pleasantly surprised. This time, God had worked fast! He said he didn't have his car but would walk me to the bus stop. He was a gentleman. He walked on the outside to protect me from the main road and anyone who might be thinking about following me. I felt like I was in heaven. I felt safe.

We had the best conversation walking up the hill. We talked until my bus came. I thanked him for looking out for me and got on the bus. When I looked in his eyes, it seemed he didn't want me to leave. But it was getting dark earlier, and I knew I needed to get home.

I got off the bus and walked home smiling. I thought about how sweet it was of Damian to walk me to the bus stop. I giggled thinking about our conversation and how funny he was.

Then I noticed Tommy's car outside Ray's house again. He must have sensed my presence because just as I walked by, he came out and walked toward his car. "What's up?" he said.

"Hey," I replied. "I thought you were supposed to meet with what's-her-name today."

"Who, Charlie?"

"Is that her name? The cheerleader chick? Your girl …."

"Yeah, well, she said she had some things to take care of today. So her friend Kelly took her home."

I was confused. *I thought she said …* Oh, *I get it.* I quickly said my goodbyes and ran into my house. I ran up to my room and turned on the computer.

Bing ….

DrDetroit: R u home safely?

DeDelicious: yes, thanks to you. U surprised me today.

DrDetroit: I think that you had the wrong impression of me.

DeDelicious: we'll see. I gotta eat and get some work done. Maybe we can chat later.

DrDetroit: K. Cant wait

I went downstairs and had dinner with my parents. I was glad to see both of them, but there seemed to be some tension in the air. All eyes turned to me. We went through the usual questions about school, boys and sports. Then it fell silent. No one had anything to say. It was awkward. I ate as quickly as I could and headed back to my room.

As I passed my desktop, I saw I had a message.

DrDetroit: Hey beautiful. Sleep well.

I smiled and laid down to rest. I couldn't stop smiling.

Damian walked me to the bus stop for the next several weeks. I found out that he was a military brat. His dad was in the Air Force and has been stationed here for the last four years. He was born in Detroit (that was why he claimed he was such a good dancer), but since then, he had lived in Colorado, Texas, Germany, and Korea. His father hoped to retire here but had recently received orders to go back to Korea. Damian said that next year he would stay in this area with his crazy aunt (his mom's sister).

His mom and dad had divorced about two years before. She moved back home to Texas. Damian said he missed his mom, but he rarely talked to her. It felt to him like she'd moved on and tried to erase his dad from her memory. And since Damian was the constant reminder of what she hated, Damian had to stay away as well.

She has since remarried and had a set of twins and one more was on the way. He joked about her needing to be the poster child for birth control, but I could sense that he was bothered by her actions. I'm sure there were many more reasons why he chose to stay with his dad. Besides, it sounded like he had a really close relationship with his dad.

Damian was kinda cool. I'd really judged him wrong. We

continued our daily afternoon walks and our evening instant messaging.

My birthday was coming soon. My parents and I finally figured out what I could do with my friends. My mom called in a favor and got us a skybox for the local basketball game. I could bring along up to fifteen friends. Of course I invited Ray and some of the other girls we had lunch with every day.

I invited Tommy and some of his boys who played basketball with us on weekends. I was sure the cheerleaders wouldn't know what to do, since their boys would be in my company this weekend. And of course I gave a special invite to Damian.

One day, when we were walking to the bus stop, I was listening to my iPod. I started dancing and shaking my bootie. I mimicked singing a song, but he couldn't figure it out. So I handed him my iPod and set it for the special MP3 message I made for him. There was the song we danced to at the Homecoming dance playing in the background, leading to a message by yours truly:

If you are listening to this message, you have received an extra special invite from the Birthday Girl. I would love for you, Mr. number 38, Mr. Homecoming Prince, my Protector and Friend, to escort me to my fifteenth birthday party at the D.C. Arena when the Wizards take on the Heat! Can't wait to see you there.

Damian smiled once he heard my message. He nodded yes and gave me the tightest, warmest hug. He was a sweetheart for walking me every day and making sure I got home safe. This was the least I could do.

Go DeDe- It's my birthday!

We all made it to the game on time. No one wanted to miss the Wizards versus the Miami Heat. I was trying not to stare at Damian, but he looked so damn good. After calming my hormones down, I spent the half hour before the game making sure that my friends were catered to. We had drinks, food, big number-one fingers, and pretty much anything we wanted.

When the game started, I turned my attention to the court. The announcer was calling the starting lineup. I made everyone be quiet when he called Number 23. "Yeah, that's my future baby daddy, yaw." I laughed and gave Ray a high five. "If I was a little older, I would have *him* for my birthday." All the girls broke out laughing. They knew what I was talking about, but Damian and my dad just gave me "the look" and shook their heads.

"Why all the nice guys gotta be baby daddies? That's what's wrong with you girls nowadays!"

"It's a figure of speech. Chill, man. It's not to be taken seriously." I smiled, but Dad still looked disturbed. I was not going to let him ruin my night. So I turned my attention to the court.

Then I heard a comment: "He wouldn't want you as a baby mama no way!"

"Excuse me?" I turned around and saw Tommy laughing with his crew.

"Yeah, one look at your mug in the morning—he wouldn't want his baby to look like that!"

"Oh yeah, our baby will look better than yours and Charlie's."

Oh shit. It just slipped out. Everyone was silent. They looked at both of us. I tried to laugh, but I think they caught on that I wasn't joking. He looked at me like he could have killed me. Then he looked at Ray. All she could do was put her head down.

Fortunately, the crowd roared with cheers and everyone's attention turned back to the game. A Miami player had stolen the ball, but the home team was able to get the ball back and come down the middle for a slam. The crowd went crazy. It was the last point scored before halftime.

During the break Tommy approached Ray. I could read her lips when she repeatedly said, "I did not tell her." She looked ready to cry. He just looked angry.

The game was awesome. The home team won 119–118 in overtime. After the game, we gathered our belongings and prepared to go home. All of a sudden, I looked up and saw HAPPY BIRTHDAY DEDE on the jumbotron. Then it showed different players singing happy birthday to me—the best players of the NBA. I smiled when they were done and turned to walk out. I thought the show was over.

"Hey, where are you going?" I turned around at Mr. Number 23, talking to me. "We were just getting started. You gonna join me or what?" Then the sexiest man on earth walked out on the court. I looked at my mom, hugged her and my dad, and ran down the steps from the skybox to the court. There must have been a thousand steps. It felt like it was forever before I reached courtside.

And there he stood, looking just as handsome as ever. "I heard you got skills. Show me." Then he bounce-passed me the ball. I lost the actual one-on-one game with Mr. Number 23, but I didn't care. I played ball with Number 23, and he gave me some basketball tips! How many people that I know, can say that? Just like homecoming, I could not stop talking all the way home.

DrDetroit: Good night, birthday girl. Hope I didn't spoil your day. You're very special and deserve nothing but the best. Can't wait to walk you home on Monday.

Ray and Tommy did not speak to me for a few weeks. At first I was bothered by it. What did Ray have to do with any of this? *Why is she choosing him over me? I'm supposed to be her best friend.*

When Christmas break began, I took the time to start my training for the softball season. I figured I needed to stay in shape because there was no way I was missing basketball season next year. I took daily jogs throughout the neighborhood.

One day when I was running, I saw Tommy. I had to talk to him. I needed forgiveness for telling his business the way I did on my birthday. I walked toward him, and he tried to walk away. I called his name and yelled my apology.

He turned and looked into my eyes as if he could see right through me. He asked me how I'd found out about Charlie being pregnant. He looked like he wanted to cry. He was so upset. He said Charlie kept pressuring him to have sex without protection. She wanted to have the baby. He was beginning to realize he was not ready to be a father. He wanted to play sports. He wanted to date other women. He wanted to be a child. I told him "When you make adult decisions, you have to accept the adult circumstances."

"You sound like my parents."

"You told them?"

"No, but I know that's what they would say. The only person I told was Ray. By the way, you never said how you found out"

I was scared to tell him, but I knew he needed to know. "Tommy, I don't know how to tell you this. But the baby may not be yours." He looked very confused, and I began to tell him about what happened in the bathroom. "I'm sorry to have to tell you this, but I think she's trying to play you."

"Damn," he said. "I knew that witch was a little too nice."

"Well, you weren't calling her a witch ten minutes ago. So be smart about it, and don't start calling her names now. Besides, she could not have gotten where she is if you didn't participate!"

"So what am I supposed to do, be happy?"

"At least act like it until we figure this out!"

"You mean you're gonna help me?"

"I've been waiting to get that heifer back since I met her. Nothing would be sweeter."

The next Monday Ray, Tommy, and I met to discuss the situation. We all sat in Ray's family room trying to figure out what to do. Ray and Tommy were acting kind of strange, but I tried to not acknowledge it because we were here to fix that jezebel Charlie.

Apparently, they had been trying to investigate this pregnancy over the last few weeks. So I was confused on whether they'd brought me into this plan as a friend to help or to use me as a pawn in their game.

Through conversations with their parents, Ray and Tommy found out that Charlie's dad worked for my dad. They needed some kind of access to Charlie outside of school, and I was the key. They planned to get even with her at the company Christmas party coming up for employees and their families. That was where the plan truly started.

We met and prepared for an entire week. I felt like I was in some type of *Mission: Impossible* movie. I had to learn the names and faces of employees and relatives of Charlie, exits to the building, and even stuff about the technology department (where Charlie's father worked). I don't know who their source was, but Ray and Tommy had plans to the building where the party was taking place, copies of the program and even seating charts of all the guests.

I felt bad for Damian because I dropped that bomb about Tommy at my birthday party. He did not catch on, and now I was hiding this big secret from him. I was sworn to secrecy. I kept quiet because I figured this was the least I could do to make up for causing the scene at my party. And at this point, if they were making these elaborate plans to trap Charlie, who knows what they know about me or what they would do to me. I knew I did not like Charlie, but still, something did not feel right about this Christmas party.

Damian and I kept on with our afternoon walks to the bus stop, but our evening online conversations were very short because I spent about an hour at Ray's house every night and then came home and did my homework. He asked me if I was okay or if I wanted to talk to him about something, but I just told him that academically, this was a busy time for me because two teachers wanted major projects completed before the holiday. I didn't lie to him. I had a Science project and English report due in a week. I just left out my secret meetings with our friends nightly.

<u>The Christmas Party</u>

The night of the Christmas party finally arrived. I had on the most beautiful red and black dress. My hair was in an updo which showed off my neckline and the necklace my father gave me my second Christmas at my grandmother's house.

I was so nervous. My palms were sweaty, my heart was pounding and I could not sit down. A million thoughts were floating through my head. This was too much pressure for a fifteen-year-old. As I was leaving the house, I saw Tommy and Ray in her window giving me the thumbs-up signal. Everything was ready to go.

I arrived at the party right on time. The first hour I would spend mingling with the executives. I dazzled them with my expertise and knowledge of the company. I felt like a star. At exactly 7:30, I excused myself and went to look for Charlie. As I left, I could hear people compliment my father on raising such a beautiful, intelligent, and well-mannered daughter. I was glad I could make him proud.

It took me a little while to find her, but when I finally did, she was unrecognizable. She barely had on any makeup and was fully covered. What happened to Miss Thang, who always had to look the best? Her mouth dropped open when she saw me. She definitely did not expect me to be there. It looked like she wanted to crawl under a rock and hide. Her parents looked very plain—borderline homely. No one would even guess that they were her parents, based on the way she dressed and acted at school. She already looked embarrassed, but I wasn't going to let her off that easily.

Time was flying by. When the program reached the point where they were presenting Christmas bonuses and awards, I snuck to the back door to let Ray and Tommy in. You could hear the clapping coming from the main ballroom. Then Tommy called Charlie on her cell phone. We saw her walk into the hallway to have a conversation.

Ray was dressed like a thief in the night. She wore a black shirt and pants, boots and a black knit hat. I think she was taking this "mission impossible" a little too far. She cracked her knuckles like she was ready to do some damage.

We started to walk toward Charlie when I saw my mom come through the doors. She called for me and told me to come see my father get his award. She also said she had a big surprise for me.

I walked back to my seat and I saw my brother sitting in the chair next to mine. He was wearing a tux. I ran and gave him the biggest hug. I hadn't seen him since the incident with Chuck. Actually, he was leaving for college at the same time, but I couldn't remember which came first. I was excited. I couldn't stop hugging him and smiling.

My dad walked up to accept his award. Everyone loved him. His employees were screaming and whistling as they gave him a standing ovation. He spoke to everyone about dreams. He told his story of being older and unemployed and how the company had taken a chance on him.

You could see that he was inspiring the staff and their families. My dad was a hero and a leader. Although he was showing gratitude to the company for giving him a chance, they were saluting him for being an awesome employee and human being.

Then during a pause in his speech, a scream came from the back of the room. Charlie stumbled in, crying, bleeding, and holding her stomach. She reached out for anyone to help her. My brother was the first one to run to her side. "Baby, are you okay?"

Baby? What the hell did he mean by that?

"Someone get a doctor!" he yelled.

The room became chaotic. People were screaming and running in a mass panic. My parents tried to move the crowd that formed around Charlie back to their seats. The paramedics had been called and were on their way. I ran out to make sure that Ray and Tommy were nowhere to be found. I didn't find them.

My brother repeated, "Baby, are you okay? What happened?" Charlie looked in my direction and shed a tear. The paramedics stormed in and took over. Then my brother yelled, "Be careful. She's carrying our baby!" I almost fainted. *I know he didn't say what I thought he said.* All of a sudden the room started spinning, and I blacked out.

When I woke up, I heard my brother calling my name. I opened my eyes and saw Mom leaning over me with tears in her eyes. I felt a little groggy but was able to stand up with help from my father and brother. I hoped that I was waking from a dream but it wasn't. My brother kissed my mother and said he had to get to the hospital.

So many things were running through my head. Did Ray and Tommy know that the other man was my brother? What did they do to Charlie that made her bleed so badly? Blood was not part of the plan. We were supposed to scare the girl into the truth, not hurt her.

I got home and rushed to my phone. I called Ray. No one answered. I was pissed. I left her a voicemail: *"Ray, call me asap."*

I couldn't sleep at all that night. I tossed and turned. Thoughts of Charlie running into the room haunted my thoughts. *Oh my God, what did I do?*

I heard my brother come into the house at around 4:00 in the morning. It sounded like he was still sniffling. I walked to his room and gave him a big hug. After crying for about twenty minutes, he just started talking. He told me the whole story.

After Chuck was killed, he knew he had to leave. Apparently he was with my cousin Angie when everything went down. He found out after some hours of threatening people what Chuck had done to me. He knew what he had to do to protect me. Once they killed him, he went to college the way he was supposed to. He knew no one would snitch because they knew he would come back for them if they did.

Anyway, he started a new life at college. He went to all his classes, went to a few college parties, and began giving tours on campus. He knew his life was changing for the better. One weekend while giving tours, he met Charlie. He talked about how sweet and innocent she seemed. He met her mom and just knew this was the girl for him. They dated for a few months, and then he decided that she was the only girl for him.

They decided to take things to the next level. Not only were they supposed to be exclusive, but they also decided to have sex. The next thing he knew, she was calling him saying she was pregnant. He genuinely loved her and wanted to do what was right. He wanted to marry her. He reached into his luggage and pulled out the gold band he was going to give her.

As I held it, I began to cry. I had to tell him.

I spilled my guts. I told him she was just a sophomore at my school. Girls feared and hated her because she was a cheerleader. I went to my room to show him her homecoming flyer. He couldn't believe this was his girl. I told him about Tommy, her boyfriend, how whorish she acted when she was at the mall, and how cruel she was to me at school. I knew that he didn't want to believe me, but I had no reason to lie.

I went on telling him how she wanted Tommy to pay for the abortion, but I told Tommy about her having someone else. "How did you know?" my brother asked. I told him I didn't know it was him, but I overheard the conversation in the bathroom when she was telling someone else that he was the only one in her life. That someone must have been my brother.

He was angry, but I don't think he knew where to direct that anger. I took a deep breath and told him to sit down because there was more. I told him about our mission that night. We had devised a plan to scare her into telling Tommy the truth and for him to break up with her. The plan changed when Mom called me into the main room, and I didn't know what had happened after that. I started crying. My brother pulled me close to comfort me. I knew it had to be hard for him to be hugging me. After all, I was technically part of the reason why he might have lost a baby that was possibly his.

We fell asleep in his room, he in his bed and I in the chair near the window. We woke up startled by a banging on the front door. We went to the window and could see a shadow of a man pacing back and forth. He was looking in the windows to see who was in the house and then started pacing again. He started screaming at the top of his lungs. "Where is he? Boy, you better come out here right now!" Boom. Boom. Boom. Boom. Boom. He banged on the door some more. My father opened the door to see who was crazy enough to bang on our door at this time in the morning. It was Charlie's dad.

He looked at my father. "You think you're so high and mighty. You're sitting up there giving your speech that was so inspiring to us little people while your son is off gallivanting with fifteen-year-olds." He pulled out a gun.

My father stepped back leaving room for Charlie's father to step aggressively in the house. My brother ran downstairs and stood face-to-face with the gun. He showed no fear. He had faced many guns in his life, so he knew how to handle this one. "I'm sorry, sir. I'm just as upset as you are. I didn't know she was fifteen. According to your wife, who damn near set us up, she was eighteen and looking for colleges."

"My wife? I don't understand."

"Well, you see, sir, last October your wife and daughter came to visit my school. They asked specifically to be on my tour. Damn, I *was* set up, wasn't I? This was planned! You knew—" My brother looked Charlie's father straight in the eyes. His hand started trembling. He grabbed the gun out of the man's hand, and Charlie's father fell to his knees.

"We didn't expect her to get pregnant. We wanted you to get in trouble for being with a minor. That way your father, Mr. Goody-Goody, would pay for denying me a promotion while he sits in his corner office making more money than any of us."

"That's what this is about?" My father was so angry you could see veins pop out of his head. He reached for Charlie's father like he was going to strangle him. It took all our might, but my brother and I were able to hold him back. "Your job is the least of your worries right now!" My brother kept Charlie's father on his knees at gunpoint, while Dad went to the kitchen and called the police. When they arrived, they took her father away in handcuffs.

Hours later, they came for my brother. Apparently while her dad was at our house making a scene, Charlie's mother was at the hospital claiming that her daughter had been taken advantage of and mentioned my brother's name.

I was so upset, I needed to get out. Around 8:00 in the morning I called Damian. He was the only one that I trusted. I needed to see his smile.

I headed out on my bike. The neighborhood seemed quiet and strange. There was always someone outside in their yard or at least ready to wave back as they left their driveway. Today, there was no one.

I met Damian at the park. He said I'd called right on time; he just got his car back. I was glad. We were able to drive around and keep warm. We pulled into an old drive-in movie parking lot. He sensed by my silence that something was wrong. I wanted to tell him, but I just couldn't. Tears started running down my face. He leaned over and gave me the biggest hug.

I mumbled, "My brother has been set up! And there's not a damn thing I can do. He has always been there for me. It's not fair. He just got a second chance to do right."

"What happened, DeDe?" His voice oozed compassion. I told him everything, starting when I heard that phone conversation in the bathroom. Then I told him what happened after my birthday and the "meeting of the minds." I told him how we came up with a plan to scare Charlie into telling Tommy the truth. I went on to describe Ray and how she was acting funny. She was so protective of him. "So you don't know?" he asked.

"Know what?"

"That Ray and Tommy used to go out last year until …."

"Don't stop now. Until what?"

"Until they found out that they were brother and sister." Apparently Ray's dad was having a good year with both of their mothers. Their father had to sit them down after he caught them kissing in the bedroom. If Tommy wasn't his son, he would have been dead. Anyway, Ray has sworn that no girl can have him. She hated Charlie for more reasons than Charlie being a cheerleader and homecoming princess. I'm sorry you got pulled into this. I wonder if they knew the other man is your brother."

"I've been wondering that myself," I replied. "They researched that her father worked for my father. Who knows what else they knew? This whole thing is crazy!"

"Well, I'm glad you're okay. I can deal with some craziness, but I don't know what I would do if something happened to you." He brushed my bangs to the side and leaned over and kissed me. It was so real and passionate, I felt it down to my toes. It was one of those old-fashioned movies type kiss, where the man grabs the girl before she can even speak any more words. Damian was too good to be true.

I felt like a peasant girl who turned into a princess in the fairy tale. Who knew this crazy jokester would be my knight in shining armor? *It's a shame I can't date yet.* He would be the first guy I would ever bring home to the family. I hated to end this, but the reality was that I had family at home going through a crisis.

I had to figure out how I was going to fix this. So I started with Charlie. On Monday morning, when everyone came back to school after a long Christmas break, flyers were hanging everywhere—Charlie's homecoming flyers (with a few little additions). I added a picture of her daddy wearing a jail suit and her mother holding thousands of dollars in her hands. The caption said: "Which side does this princess take after, the jailbird father or the money-hungry whore mother?" The words *money-hungry whore* were circled.

Everyone was staring at her and laughing as she walked down the hall. I followed her. I had to see her face. She ran into the bathroom. I walked in after her. I kicked open the stall and said, "Now you know how it feels, wench. And I'm just getting started. Come near me or my family again, and you …." I stared at her until I couldn't bare to see her face any more. I walked out of the bathroom, not caring about her or her family's feelings.

She stayed clear of me after that. Her reputation was trashed at our school and at the surrounding boys' schools. The varsity cheer captain kicked her off the squad because she was tarnishing the names of all cheerleaders. She was no longer popular; she had no friends and no followers. She had absolutely nothing left.

Miraculously, her mother dropped the charges against my brother. Unfortunately, the state's attorney wouldn't. Even with the DNA proof that the baby wasn't his and their sex was consensual, he'd still had sex with a minor. My daddy promised my brother that he would get him out soon. I agreed. I couldn't see my family in any more pain.

I kept a low profile. My grades were still high. I made honor roll again. Even with all that my family had been through, they took time to celebrate my academic accomplishments. I appreciate them more than they could know.

Chapter 4

Quarter 3

I spent every day with Damian after school and on weekends. We did everything from playing basketball and going to the mall and kissing in the park. He was truly sweet and kind, a perfect gentleman ... just like my daddy. I felt as if he was my only friend.

I visited my brother every weekend in jail. He seemed happy but I could tell he just wanted to run out of the place. Fortunately he was able to wear his own clothes. Those orange jumpsuits with the numbers printed on it did nothing for his great sense of style. The walls of the visiting room were gray and stale looking. There were no beautiful designs, patterns, or even signs of life. There was nothing but the basic furniture—black chairs and black tables and they were bolted to the ground.

My nights were spent dreaming of the day my brother would be released from jail and how I was going to get Ray and Tommy back. In my heart, I believed they knew everything about my brother; and even if they didn't know about him, look where their plan got him. After watching what they did to Charlie, I couldn't put anything past the two of them. I still couldn't figure out how I was going to find out the truth. So I decided since they'd investigated me, I would investigate them.

Ray walked around school as if nothing had happened. Tommy picked up where he left off but with another cheerleader. *Poor thing, she doesn't even have a clue. She is never going to get anywhere with him, at least not if Ray can help it.*

I played their game too. I smiled in their faces, had fake conversations and even hung at her house a few nights. I knew that things would never be the same. But I still needed to know their version of the truth.

<u>It's time....</u>

The third Saturday in February, we went to my grandmother's house. Her birthday was actually on Valentine's Day. Everyone was so busy with our day-to-day activities that no one in the family was able to celebrate her birthday until the weekend. My parents made sure that we were free that weekend to celebrate.

When we walked in her house, the whole place fell quiet. It was like nobody knew what to say to us because of my brother being locked up. My mom walked over to my grandma and gave her a hug and kiss that swept her off her feet. Mommy hugged her so tight, my grandmother sounded like she was gasping for air. This made everyone laugh. My mom's gesture seemed to have put the family at ease.

After an hour of socializing, I slid out the back door. Angie saw me and followed me. I had not spoken to her since we left Grandma's house months ago. She stopped and looked at me like she wanted to say something but I didn't need to hear any words. We gave each other a hug; regardless of how we act, we are still family.

She walked with me the few blocks to my brother's friend Antoine's house. The last time I went to visit my brother, I told him that I needed to find out what really happened. Ty tried to discourage me, but I refused to listen. I guess he realized I was not going to give up. So he gave me the number to call his buddy Antoine. Antoine was one of Ty's closest friends on the street. Most of the nights where Ty did not come in until after curfew, he was with Antoine. He knew that Antoine had "special skills" that no one else had and he would do anything if my brother asked.

When you walk into Antoine's house, you would think that an elderly person lives there. There was that hard, thick plastic over the pinkish paisley designed furniture and lots of family pictures, and the smell of Sunday dinner permeated the air. The hallway was narrow and kind of plain. The walls had wood paneling and without the light, it looked like a long tunnel. The carpet was a tan color with a plastic runner on top. I guess that was to keep all of the tracks from people's shoes off of his carpet.

We walked to the back of the house, and it was totally different. It was as if I had just morphed into another time period. I looked as if this part of the house was just built. Everything was white, smooth and clean. We walked in the first room on the right. There was state-of-the-art technology all over (laptops, the latest desktops with multiple monitors, flat screen tvs hanging from the walls, the works!). I felt like I was a part of one of my favorite detective TV shows- The Last 48 or CSI. There were photographs hanging on the wall. Someone had been watching everything that I was doing. There were pictures of me playing basketball, me at school and pictures of me with Damian. When I saw those pictures, I felt like my face was turning red with embarrassment. And I also felt warm thinking of those special moments with Damian.

I saw several pictures of Ray and her family. And then I saw pictures of Tommy and his family. I saw pictures of Ray's mom talking and in some pictures it looked like she was arguing with Tommy's dad. I was amazed by the photography. It was like someone was following their every move. You could see facial expressions and emotions. Clearly there was something going on in this family.

Then my eyes were drawn to a computer screen. A phone call was coming through on Ray's cell phone. It was Tommy. Dang, this guy was good. I didn't even want to know how he was able to tap into the cell phone, but this was indisputable evidence that there is no privacy in this world. The call was short, but they planned on meeting up soon. They gave a place and a time. At that point, Antoine radioed someone to pass on the place and time. I was impressed.

He walked me over to another wall and plotted out their family tree. It included names, pictures, jobs for the last ten years, lovers, and medical histories. Come to find out that Ray's and Tommy's father had been spreading the fruit of his loins (If you know what I mean). He had twelve children altogether. I wondered if Ray and Tommy knew about their siblings. I looked more closely at the wall and read that Ray's father had tested positive for HIV in December—exactly two weeks before the Christmas party.

Based on their conversations, they knew that Charlie was messing with a college boy but did not know who. At the time of Ray beating Charlie, her emotions were heightened by her dad and mom arguing about him having HIV and how she might have contracted it from him after a recent rendezvous they'd had the month before. I could only imagine what Ray was going through and for a quick moment, I felt bad for her. But she had crossed the line when she investigated and hurt my family. Best friend or not, she would have to come to terms with what she had done.

This was a lot of information to take in. I had to think of what I was going to do with it. Angie was quiet on the walk back to Grandma's house. I could see in her face she wanted to do something. It was probably the same expression she had when she found out what Chuck did to me. I turned to her and told her I had this one under control. I didn't want to have another situation on her conscience. This one I wanted to handle myself.

When we went back to my grandmother's house, it was like we had never left. People were still talking and catching up on the weekly gossip. The only person who noticed I'd been gone was my mom. She gave me that look, like she knew I was up to something. I just brushed it off and acted like I was there the whole time.

Days later, I still could not figure out how to handle this. I couldn't be mad at Ray and Tommy because they didn't know my brother was the other man. But there had to be a way for them to help me get my brother's case thrown out.

I saw my brother the following weekend. His spirits were always high. I didn't know if it was a façade for me or if that was how he really felt. We talked about school and about what Antoine had found out. I needed him to help me. I was truly stuck. We felt bad because their family had already been affected (or should I say infected) by their father's actions.

My brother tried to act brave and told me to leave it alone. I couldn't believe what he was saying. He referenced a podcast he was listening to the night before. There was a part where this woman who was preaching said, if she wanted to move on with her life, she had to let the anger go; if she stayed angry, then she would be stuck where she was—miserable. He told me he forgave me for my role in all of this, but now the focus needed to be on getting him out.

He was right. My brother's freedom came before trying to get revenge on people. He gave me a hug, and at that moment, in my mind, I let go. I let go of my anger toward Ray and Tommy. I let go of my anger toward Charlie and her family. I let go of being mad at myself and blaming myself for what had happened to my brother.

When I got home, I went outside to put in my usual workout time. I knew I needed to stay in shape for the next basketball season. So this spring I tried out for softball and made the team. I have always been a competitive person and softball was just up my alley. It kept me physically fit and helped me rebuild my stamina. My parents seemed a little apprehensive about me playing. Just because I was awesome in basketball, did not necessarily mean I would be good at another sport. They knew I was a highly competitive athlete. But those thoughts were totally dismissed when they came to one of my games. I was a little nervous because Damian was also in the crowd that day. He hadn't missed any of my games. We beat the other team badly, 13–4. I was named the MVP of the game and was given the game ball.

I ran over and gave Damian a hug. He surprised me and brought his dad to the game. We exchanged smiles and handshakes. He said he had heard so much about me that he just had to meet me. Those compliments made me blush because I knew they could have only come from one person… Damian. *I wonder what else he told him?*

I walked Damian and his dad over and formally introduced them to my parents, who didn't look mad or worried. I was surprised. They knew about Damian but were glad that I had enough respect for them to introduce him and his dad. We all wanted to go out to celebrate my victory and MVP status, so my dad invited Damian and his father out to lunch.

We had a great time talking over lunch and desserts. My dad retired from the military, so those guys had a lot to talk about. Of course they took turns bragging about who was a better athlete, me or Damian. Damian's dad bragged about Damian's athleticism, academics, and future plans. My dad bragged about my academics. He said he would talk about my athleticism, but Damian's dad had seen the game. It spoke for itself. They let out a big laugh. Both of them talked lots of junk! Damian's dad was really cool. Everyone seemed to be having fun.

Before we started to leave, Damian excused himself and said he needed to get something from the truck. When he reappeared, he walked in with a silly grin and one hand hiding something behind his back. He got down on one knee and pulled a corsage from behind his back. "DeDe, will you go to the prom with me?"

I just froze. I didn't know what to say. My parents don't even let me date. I turned around to look at their faces and to get their approval. My mom looked like she wanted to be in my shoes. She had that "Oh, that's so romantic" look on her face. Dad gave me an approving nod and the "Don't make me regret this" look.

"*Yes! Yes*. Yes," I said as he slid the corsage on my wrist. Everyone on our side of the restaurant started screaming and clapping. Our dads shook hands, exchanged information (phone numbers and emails), and decided it was time to go home.

When we pulled up to the house, I noticed something different in the neighborhood. Ray's house had a for-sale sign on the front lawn. The house looked empty and quiet, even though I knew they were still living there. I saw Ray in her window watching our family car pull into the garage. I tried calling her phone, but the house phone and cell phone were disconnected. I caught her online.

DeDelicious: Please don't get offline. You're moving?

Sunshyne: Yes, we have to move. Monday, I start my new school. The headmaster of the new school is a friend of my mom's.

DeDelicious: I know this may not really help but I'm sorry. I want you to know that if you need anything, I'm here for you.

Sunshyne: You don't even know half of it.

DeDelicious: I'm afraid I do. I know about your mom and dad. I know your dad is sick.

There was a long pause in between messages.

Sunshyne: She disconnected the phones.

He's been begging to talk to my mom.

He swore he didn't know that he had contracted the disease. My mom had to get a restraining order to stop him from coming over.

After all of these problems he has caused, I honestly don't think he knows how many people he has infected by not only being promiscuous but selfish.

My mom put me in counseling.

I didn't want to go at first but I'm glad I did.

I realize why I've done these terrible things because I was hurt.

The main reason is because I've never talked to anyone about anything going on in my life.

I covered it up and buried myself in school work and activities all the time.

I felt like she had been holding so much in. She needed a friend right now.

DeDelicious: Well I'm glad you're getting help.

For some reason, people of color refuse to let someone help us. So it is awesome that you are seeing a psychologist.

Sunshyne: Dede, thank you for being a friend.

You've been nothing but a friend especially when you could have put out my family's business.
But you've been holding out too!
I didn't know you and D were like that!

DeDelicious: We're cool. Just friends.

I didn't want the conversation to turn out to be about me.

Sunshyne: Well, I gotta finish packing.

This is my last night here.
As soon as I get the new address, I'll email you.

DeDelicious: Take care of yourself.

Sunshyne: Take care of you. Peace and Blessings.

Her avatar disappeared from my screen. I closed my eyes and gave a quick prayer, hoping she would be okay. When I opened my eyes, I began to search the net. I decided to look for prom dresses. I couldn't believe that Damian had asked me to go to his prom. I tried to play it cool, but inside I was ready to explode.

As time for the prom drew nearer, you could detect a change in focus. In health classes the focus went from learning about topics like anxiety nd depression to the effects of drugs and alcohol and (my favorites) sex and pregnancy.

My mom also took the opportunity to talk to me about sex.

We'd had many talks before. My mom was kinda cool to talk to. When I was about eight years old, she took the time to talk to me about changes in my body and the difference between boys and girls. When I was ten, she took the time to talk about how babies are created and how it's easier to make them than to raise them. At thirteen, I learned from her about sexually transmitted diseases (STDs) and how they occur in nearly two-thirds of those under the age of twenty-five because they are constantly having unprotected sex and with multiple partners. She always stressed how important it is to be responsible. She was always open and honest with me, which in turn made me always willing to listen and have a conversation with her.

Things did change when I was raped by Chuck. My mom had told me that my first time would not be easy and possibly painful, but who would have thought that that would happen to me—and with a person my family trusted? Although she understood that I'd already had a sexual experience (a horrific one at that), she tried to instill in me that I needed to make appropriate decisions.

Most recently my mom talked to me about intimacy. She wanted me to know that sex is a beautiful experience that must not be exploited negatively. She told me how important it is to take the time to get to know your partner because you two will be taking care of each other. Social pressures influence people (not just teens) toward unsafe practices, like not using condoms. Her goal was to make sure I was safe at all times.

And most of all, sex is a trust issue. Trust is a way of being safe and not getting pregnant. You have to know that whoever you choose to lay with, has your back. Trust is being safe and not passing around STD's. Trust is having open and clear communication. Trust is saying no when you're not ready and respecting your partner's wishes. Trust is being there for your partner the day after.

My mother's talk meant a lot to me. I didn't see it as lecturing me or making me feel like I couldn't make a good decision. She asked me questions. She asked me how I felt physically and asked me about my emotions. I was honest. I know there were some things my mother didn't want to hear, but she wanted me to share my thoughts rather than hide them from her. I think she was highly protective, especially after what happened with Chuck.

My dad hung in the background. His talks were a little different. He constantly warned me about boys. He tried not to push too hard because of what I had been through. Daddy knew that I was not going to give it up to just any guy, but he understood that teens have urges. He tried to tell me to have expectations about what type of boy I wanted to deal with and, most importantly, not to deviate from what I knew was best for me. He often tried to model behaviors and manners that a guy I date should have, like opening doors and making me walk on the inside of the sidewalk so he could protect me.

Daddy told me some guys are sincere, but a lot of them are out just to conquer the girl (i.e., to get another notch on their belt or get the booty). Some boys may stop at nothing to get girls to have sex with them. Some may pay you like a prostitute (by giving you money and clothes), some may compliment you (ya know, make you feel real good, you cute), and some may ignore you- so that you can "chase" them. There are many ways to prey on girls. Daddy let me know all the tricks so that I wouldn't fall for any of them. He told me to focus on me. Take care of myself and my schoolwork, and decide what I want to do with my life; the boys will always be there. Daddy always ended with "Just love you, baby girl."

While everyone was spending every waking moment preparing for prom, I was praying for my brother's court date. I had been to see him every weekend since he was put in jail. I always made sure he was well taken care of and had everything he needed. He had the latest clothes, all his toiletries, and every commodity that could be used to barter.

The weekend before the trial he was very happy. He had just met with his lawyer, and the outlook seemed promising. I had asked him what he wanted to do when he came home. He told me he wanted to have dinner with the whole family.

He told me that he loved me for everything I did for him. To me, it was the least I could do. When he took care of Chuck, he gave me peace. Now it's my chance to do the same.

Judgement Day...

We walked in the courtroom Monday morning. My stomach was turning, and I felt sick. He actually looked quite handsome in his black three-piece suit and royal blue shirt underneath. He walked across the room to take his seat next to his lawyer. My brother was going to be sitting in the seat of thousands of criminals, rapists, and convicted murderers. My brother's innocence would be tested. The prosecutor began his opening statement. He tried his best to make my brother look like some type of serial rapist for one incident of consensual sex. My brother's attorney portrayed my brother as an innocent college student preyed upon by an entire family in order to seek a father's revenge. Our entire family was there to support him and fight this injustice. We all wore white as a symbol of unity and a peaceful ending.

I tried to watch the judge's face as both sides gave their evidence, questioned witnesses, and eloquently posed closing arguments. There were two full days of testimony, including the testimony of Charlie and her crazy mother. Charlie cried on the stand, begging that my brother be released. At one point in her testimony, she tried to make everyone feel bad for her. I never felt bad for those fake tears and the sad stories she told. That slut had destroyed my brother and my family.

I prayed that this judge didn't want to make an example out of my brother, like the young man from Atlanta who was sentenced to ten years for having oral sex performed on him by an underage girl. What was absurd about that case was that he was underage too! When I heard about him, I couldn't believe that such a thing could happen to a young African American male who had the world ahead of him—college and opportunity. The girl also did it willingly. Charlie and her mother spoke during the trial on Ty's behalf. He was one of the most popular people in school, an honor roll student that had scholarship offers from several colleges around the nation.

We knew this was not going to be an easy battle for my brother, even the young man in Atlanta's family had to solicit to get political resources involved in order to get laws changed for his release. But the system used that young man as an example for every male. It had been two years. Anyone could see that was wrong. *Would this person who went in as a boy and would come out a man ever fit into society? Where was the justice?*

The two hours of deliberation felt like years. When they told us the verdict was in, my entire body felt heavy. I closed my eyes and kept my head in my hand and prayed as the judge read the verdict.

My brother was found NOT GUILTY. Screams were heard across the courtroom. My mother and I had tears in our eyes. We all ran up to embrace my brother. We held on to him as if we would never let go ever again. We gave hugs to his attorney, and if we could have, we would have hugged the judge too. Thank you, God!

That night we filled up an entire section of my brothers favorite restaurant to celebrate him. Family members who were usually too busy during the week came out. My brother's true friends came out. Damian and his dad came out. All together, there were thirty seven happy faces celebrating my brother.

Everything was perfect. My brother was home, Ray was getting help and in a better place, my family was happy, grades were good, and now it was time for me to finally be the Belle of the Ball!

Chapter 5
Quarter 4

Beauty and the Beast

It was the night before the prom. I couldn't sleep at all. I decided to get up and return a few emails, do a little work on my science fair project, and anything else that would help me fall asleep. My father walked by and saw my light on. "Can't sleep?" he smirked.

"Yeah." I guess my excitement showed.

"Well, don't stay up too late. You have a long day tomorrow."

"I know." I finished typing, turned off my lamp, and returned to bed. I lay for a little while staring at the ceiling. Eventually I drifted off to sleep.

My mom let me take off from school on Friday so that we could get another pampered spa day. I really loved spending time with my mother. I don't really get a lot of alone time with her since she started her own business. The spa day gave us a chance to talk and learn about each other. I used to think she was always prying into my business when she constantly asked me about school, my friends, and boys, but I found out by talking to her that she was genuinely interested in what was going on in my life. And for the most part, she had pretty good advice if I had any concerns.

She had high expectations for me; sometimes they felt too high. But I realized she only wanted the best for me. She wanted me to have every opportunity in life that I could have. Mommy insisted that I become well educated and ahead of the curve because I was a beautiful, intelligent and athletic African American female. She wanted me to be able to ask questions and talk to her, so that I would not end up like Ray and Tommy. So each time we got "girl time" I appreciated it.

I knew I would be the most beautiful girl at the prom. The hairdresser pinned my hair up with sparkling rhinestone bobby pins. I looked so glamorous; like I was straight out of a magazine. I was beyond my usual princess status. I was working on being a queen ... Damian's Queen.

Speak of the Devil

We were on our way home and saw some guy pacing outside our house. It was Tommy. He looked like a mess. He looked like he hadn't taken a shower in days. His hair and face were grimy looking. His clothes looked like he had worn them for a week.

A couple days earlier, Damian had told me that Tommy's dad's wife left after she found out his dad was cheating and was HIV positive. Since then Tommy's dad was just bringing all kinds of women to the house. Tommy did the same. I never imagined that Tommy, the most popular guy in school, would ever hit such a low place in life. He looked and acted like someone who was hooked on drugs.

I couldn't stand to see him like that. I told my mom to stop the car. She looked like she didn't want to because she didn't know what he was going to do. I held her hand and said "Mom, Tommy may have made some bad choices, but within three months, his life has been taken up from under him. No family, no girl, no baby, nothing." She nodded and unlocked the doors for me.

I walked over to him. He wouldn't stop pacing. "Where is she?" he yelled at me. "I tried to call but her cell phone is off, her email is disabled. I can't find her."

"I don't know, Tommy. The last time I talked to her was the day before she moved."

"I believed that if I ever needed her, she would be there for me. I need her. She was my best friend. She was the only one who understood my life."

"I know it's hard and you've been through a lot. But you need to understand she needs time to get herself together. Remember, she is going through a lot too!"

"I know. I know. It's just—"

"It's just that you want us to feel bad for you. Tommy, you gotta work through this. You are on the varsity football team, and you're very popular. People are going to have high expectations of you. They see you as a smart jock and a little rich boy. They will not and cannot understand what you are going through, and you have nothing to prove to anyone."

I took a breath and continued, "But you need to get yourself together. It's not going to happen in one day, but it needs to happen. No one can get you through this if you don't reach out. Some people may not care, but I want you to know, you have more people than you think behind you."

At that moment he looked up and saw my brother standing in the doorway. Tommy looked scared. He looked like he had seen a ghost. The sight of Ty terrified him. "Tommy," I asked, "would you like to come in for something to eat?" I could see he felt uncomfortable seeing my brother. But he looked like he needed to eat. "Come on." I grabbed his arm and put it around my shoulders like a wounded soldier. "Let's get something to eat."

He turned and hugged me. His embrace was so tight. It felt like an anaconda. I felt a tear on my shoulder. This guy is really suffering. I couldn't help but feel bad for him.

I didn't have much time before I needed to get ready for the prom. Everyone was quiet at dinner. No one knew what to say to Tommy. My brother broke the ice by asking him about sports. Tommy could tell that everyone was on eggshells and trying to patronize him. After eating a few more bites, Tommy abruptly got up from the table and headed for the door. "Thank you, Mr. and Mrs. Stanton, for dinner. I gotta go. Thank you, DeDe. Oh, and by the way, you look very pretty, very different than when you first moved to the area. It's a good look!"

I blushed a little. I never knew Tommy would even notice me because of all the girls he dated. It was nice to hear that compliment. "Thanks," I said as I closed the door behind him after I saw him disappear down the street.

It was time. I washed up, lotioned and put on my favorite fragrance. My mom helped me get dressed. I gently slipped my gown over my head- trying desperately not to mess up my hair. Instantly, I was transformed. Once again Mom looked like she was going to cry. Sometimes she's a little too dramatic for me. If someone walked in the room just then, they would have thought I was a bride and she was giving me away. I did my best to try and let her have her moment.

She looked out my window and saw the limousine pull up. I watched Damian step out, looking so handsome in his black slim cut tuxedo. He had a bouquet of tropical colored flowers. I covered my mouth because I wanted to scream out to the world, "I'm going to prom, and my date is so fine!"

I started to open my bedroom door and head downstairs, but my mom told me to be patient and give a guy something to look forward to. It was hard waiting because I just wanted to jump in his arms. My heart was pounding. I felt warm. I might have even been sweating. I was so excited.

Then my dad called for me. After a long dramatic pause, I opened the bedroom door, and my mom escorted me down the steps. "You are so beautiful," Damian mouthed as he stared at me. When I got to the bottom of the steps, he reached out for me. I stretched out my arm to grab his hand and he gave it a gentle kiss on the back of my hand.

He pulled the bouquet of flowers from behind his back. I was smiling so hard. As I reached for them, he turned and offered them to my mom. I was so shocked that it took me a minute to close my mouth. My mother was very flattered. I could tell that she was elated. She even giggled like a girl when she thanked him. That made me smile and think to myself, *This brotha is real smooth.*

For the next thirty minutes we took lots of pictures—with my parents, with his dad, with each other, and by ourselves. We took enough pictures to do an entire layout in any popular magazine.

Before we left, my father pulled Damian aside. I don't know exactly what he said, but I could tell by Damian's face when he returned that it was a threat. Damian cleared his throat and let everyone know we needed to get going.

We walked toward the limousine. The chauffeur opened the back door. I peeked in and saw that the back of the limousine was filled with the same flowers that he'd given my mom. I fought the urge to cry. No one had ever done anything like that for me. When he joined me in the back, I gave him the biggest hug and kiss. I felt like a real princess in a fairy tale.

"Your mom isn't the only queen in that castle. Tonight, you're not just a princess; you are my queen." I wanted to pinch myself. No guy ever acted like this or said such nice things … unless. *Wait, he must want some booty or something.* I had to stop myself.

I didn't know why I'd just had that thought. He has given me no reason to think that way. He's a good guy. And no one has ever done anything so sweet. I know that I need to appreciate what I have.

We drove around town. It was like seeing the city for the first time, even though I'd lived here my whole life. We made it Downtown. We decided to walk around before we went to the hotel for the prom. It was beautiful. The pier, the water—it was so romantic. For a moment, it felt like no one else existed but us.

Every once in a while I noticed people looking at us. One older couple walked up to us and complimented us on how well we looked. We thanked them and returned to gazing into each other's eyes.

We walked all the way to the end of the pier. He shared things about himself that he never said on our many walks to my bus stop or in our emails. He held me tight as we looked out over the water. Not a cloud was in the sky. He gave me a gentle kiss that sent chills through my body. I didn't want him to stop. Whenever he came near me, it already felt like our bodies just gravitated to one another. He always made me feel good. Mama always told me these feelings would come. I just never thought they would be with Damian.

Everyone stared as we walked into the room. I knew we looked good but I just never thought it would be like this. No one expected Damian to bring me. They expected him to bring a cheerleader, because that was what football players did. I cleared my throat and straightened my back and reminded myself that *he chose me*. He could have the cheerleader, but he chose me. He chose the girl who had always been one of the boys. He chose the one who wasn't a perfect size four. He chose the one that made him laugh by tripping on the sidewalk or on invisible objects. He chose me, and that was all that mattered.

We had amazing fun at the prom. We danced and danced, doing our thing on the dance floor once again! We laughed endlessly. He was my Prince Charming—and was actually crowned prom king that night.

We stepped out onto the ballroom balcony to look at the skyline. He stood behind me and wrapped me in his arms. I had never felt like this toward a guy. I wanted to give myself to him, but I couldn't. It was not that it wasn't a special time or that he wasn't a special person, but I was scared and not ready.

He turned me around facing him and gave me another kiss. He reached behind him and pulled out a beautiful tiara. "For you, my queen," he said with a bow and placed it on my head. I blushed and couldn't stop smiling. *He is so full of surprises.* He grabbed me by the hand, pulled me close, and began to slow dance. We danced for maybe another twenty minutes, and then he whispered that he needed to get Cinderella home before the limo turned into a pumpkin. And if I wasn't home by midnight, my dad will come searching for him!

Our limo pulled up. The smell of those flowers still hung in the air. I got in first. Damian followed right behind me.

As we were about to pull off, the left side door opened, and Tommy jumped in. He scared the mess out of me. He still looked bad. This time, on top of looking raggedy, he seemed to have been on some type of drugs. "I need to find Ray," he bellowed, shaking.

"I don't know where she is," I said, trying not to cry.

"Don't lie to me. Stop lying, *princess.*"

I was terrified. "I'm not lying. I told you earlier, I haven't talked to her since she moved. She hasn't contacted me. As soon as she does, I'll let you know. I promise."

My heart was racing. My palms were sweaty. Tommy was scaring me. I had already calmed him down once before, but this time he seemed worse.

Damian stepped in. "Leave her alone, Tommy. She hasn't done anything to you."

"You act like you don't know what's going on, D. I'm sure this heifer has told you everything."

"I'm not going to let you call her names, Tommy. She's trying to help you."

"Help me? She hasn't done anything but cause problems in my life."

"*I* caused problems in *your* life? I wasn't the one who flirted and screwed all those girls, including your sister, following in your father's footsteps. I'm not the one who flaunts himself and always has to take the spotlight. I'm not the one who concocted a plan to beat a girl down to get information from her".

It looked like he wanted to raise his hand and hit me. Damian quickly grabbed his arm and somehow moved from my right to my left side so he was between Tommy and me. Damian looked Tommy square in the eyes, so he would know that if he would lay a finger on me, Damian will defend me. A sense of courage came over me, probably because I felt protected by Damian and so I continued.

"But I am the one who participated in a stupid scheme that got my brother thrown in jail. I am the one who offered food and shelter to a so-called friend when he had a breakdown and looked crazy going back and forth in front of an empty house. And you say I am causing problems in your life? I don't need this from you, Tommy."

I called for the limo driver to pull over. When he did, Tommy got out. He turned back but had nothing to say. Damian looked surprised and a little disappointed. I'd never told him what was going on with Tommy, even though he told me about Tommy and Ray being related. I felt as though Tommy should be the one to tell him, since that was his boy. That's one of the complicated things about relationships that I don't understand. Who was supposed to tell him, the female friend he'd grown fond of and shared many secrets with, or his boy he'd known for years, played sports with, and hung out with?

Damian's look made me feel as though I'd done something wrong. I did not say a word. I lay across the seat with my head in Damian's lap. He stroked my hair softly and twirled his fingers around my curls. What a terrible ending to a beautiful night. I closed my eyes and imagined us back on the dance floor. *Damn, he is so smooth; gotta love his swag. He's fine, a little rough on the edges, experienced some serious losses in life, but stays uplifted.* Every quality a girl would want in a guy, Damian possessed. I just hoped I hadn't broken our trust or ruined our friendship.

We arrived at my house. Even with all the craziness, I didn't want this night to end. I felt bad about what had taken place. I gave him a long hug and kiss so he would know I didn't want to go. But I knew I had to. He slowly walked me to the house. When I got in, I walked straight to my room. I got undressed and tried to lie down, but Damian's face stayed in my mind. His dimples always had a way of making me smile, but tonight all I could think about was the sadness in his beautiful eyes after Tommy jumped in the car.

I decided to call his cell phone. I never called this late at night, but I figured since it was prom night, he might just answer. I let it ring five times before I hung up. I didn't know what to say for a message. I waited a few moments, got myself together, and called again. I had expected the voicemail again. Instead, a female answered. "Hello?" she said. "Helloooo?"

"Hello, is Damian there?" I stammered.

"Aw baby, he's unavailable right now," she said in a seductive voice.

"Sharon, what are you—?" It was Damian in the background.

All I heard next was the dial tone. I hung up the phone. I was stuck. I couldn't believe what had just happened. I had called him because I felt bad. I felt like I was holding back from him, and looked at what happened. I got played. He knew not to call my house phone back—better yet, not to call me ever! I couldn't sleep at all that night. When I finally did, it was morning.

I woke up to my mom screaming my name from downstairs. She sounded as if I was down the street or something. I covered my ears with pillows, but she just kept calling my name. I knew she just wanted to hear about last night. I had come in so quickly, I doubted anyone even glimpsed the back of my head.

The house phone rang. "DeDe, it's Damian."

"Tell him I'll talk to him when I get myself together," I called back down. *Meaning never.*

"He said it's important!"

"I said tell him I'll call him back."

Bing … bing … bing … bing … bing …. My email was buzzing like crazy. The instant messages were coming up one after another. I knew it was Damian trying to reach me. There was a time when I would have jumped out of bed in the middle of the night to instant message him. But this morning I had no reason to even budge. He was wrong. Just straight up wrong. I wasn't ready to talk to him.

I finally got myself together and made it down for breakfast. I wore my tiara so that I could focus on before and during the prom. My brother and mother were sitting at the table waiting to hear about everything. My mother started clapping when she saw the tiara. "You were the prom queen?" she asked.

"No" I replied. But I commenced to tell them all about the evening. I went from the flowers in the limousine to the dancing on the balcony. I totally left out the ride home.

My brother asked if he tried to push up on me. I told him that Damian was a perfect gentleman. And then I started thinking: The reason why he was a perfect gentleman was because he had another female… whoever Sharon was, to meet up with after he dropped me off. I wanted to cry. I excused myself and ran back up to my room. My instant messages were still ringing on my computer. I turned it off and sat in my window.

As I looked outside, I saw movers carrying furniture into Ray's house. After about the third truckload, two family cars pulled into the driveway. A man, a woman, and a little boy came out of the first car. A boy and a girl, who both looked around my age, came out of the other car. The girl looked cute, but the brother was *fine*! I watched him stroll from his car into the house.

I had to meet him. I had to find a way to introduce myself. So I straightened my tiara and put on my favorite Adidas sweat suit. I went to the garage and pulled out my basketball court. I dribbled hard. I didn't want to break a sweat, but I made sure that he saw me.

I saw him walk back toward his car to get some clothes from the back. That's when I went for it. I backed up and ran up for the dunk. As I reached the rim, I accidentally hooked my arm in it. I came down on my ankle. I didn't plan on falling, but it did get me the attention I wanted from the new boy next door.

He ran from his car to my side. He asked me if I was okay and introduced himself. "Hi. I'm Trevon. It looks like I'm your new neighbor." *Helloooooo, Trevon.* I blushed and introduced myself. He asked if he could take a look at my ankle. I knew it was just twisted, but he insisted.

As Trevon leaned over to examine it, Damian's car pulled up to my driveway. I could tell by the look on his face that he was not happy with what he saw. "What's up, DeDe?" he said.

"Nothing. I fell when I was going up for a shot."

"Oh, she wasn't just going up for a shot; she tried to break the backboard," Trevon interjected excitedly.

"Oh, really," said Damian. As he looked me right in my eyes.

"Man, you should have seen her body move like a gazelle. Fast, swift, smoooooth—"

"Until the gazelle dropped like a wounded—"

"Funny, Damian." I cut him off and looked at him.

"Back to your old tricks, huh Tumbles?" I hadn't heard that name since the first time I fell off my bike. I laughed at his remark.

Trevon helped me back to my feet. I wiped off my backside because I knew both of them were looking at it. Damian cleared his throat. Trevon reached out and shook my hand. "It was very nice to meet you, DeDe" He turned to Damian and put his hand out.

"D, man."

"And you too, D. See you around."

I knew my face was red. I had never seen Damian so jealous. But as I watched Trevon go back to his car, I thought about things for a minute and Damian had no right to be jealous. He was the one having some girl named Sharon answer his phone.

He abruptly turned around and walked to his car. He opened the back door and practically dragged an older woman over to me. He said "DeDe, I'd like to introduce you to … Sharon."

"Hey, sugar," Sharon said with that same seductive voice I'd heard on the phone. She reached out with long claw-like fingernails to shake hands.

I couldn't be rude, so I shook her hand. "Nice to meet you," I said in a low voice. I couldn't convince anyone that my words were sincere.

"Sharon is my aunt's friend. I went over there last night because my family had a party. I came in while they were all playing Bid Whiz. She answered my phone when I went to the bathroom."

A shadow of embarrassment came over me. I had totally overreacted to some female answering his phone. He was on his way to drop her off at home because she drank a little too much last night. But he made sure that he introduced us because he knew what I was thinking when I wouldnt answer or accept any of his calls. The only way he felt he could clear things up was to stop at my house. He gave me a kiss on the cheek, looked dead in my eyes and said "I only want you". He then walked straight to his car and pulled off. I stood in my driveway paralyzed by the gentle kiss and his words. All I could do was smile and walk back into the house.

Damian and I talked all afternoon. He came back over because he needed to talk this through face to face. He understood why I didn't want to talk to him earlier and thought it was imperative that he tell me the whole story about Sharon.

Sharon was a friend of his mother and aunt. She had always found Damian to be very attractive. Every time she saw him, she told him that she wanted him.The fact that she was almost twenty years older than him didn't matter to her. She would make advances, stand in his space, brush up against him, and sometimes even grab his hand and put them between her legs or on her breast. Apparently for years, she had tried to get him to sleep with her. He swore on his life that he had no desire to be with her, but she promised to stop at nothing until she got a taste of him. I teased him and told him he just needed to give it up, and maybe she'd move on. We laughed for a quick moment, and then there was an odd silence.

He could see I was getting tired so he left. I went into the house. I went up to my room and laid across the bed. My phone buzzed. It was Damian. I guess he misses me already… the whole fifteen minutes since we have been apart.

"So what's the deal with you and your new neighbor?" he said.

"What do you mean?" I asked, hoping I could get away with it.

"DeDe, I'm not dumb. I haven't even seen that Adidas sweat suit since homecoming week." That made me smile. I can't believe he remembered exactly when I wore that outfit! I must have left a good impression.

"I was just playing some ball."

"With a tiara?"

Okay, now that felt awkward. He'd got me, figured out my stupid little plan. *So what do I do now?* I tried to get off the topic. He let me move on, but I knew we weren't done with that conversation. We stayed on the phone until 2:00 in the morning.

Just as I hung up, I heard a lot of screaming that came from outside the window. I went over to look, and it was Tommy standing outside Ray's old house. He was throwing rocks at the window that was once hers and yelling at the top of his lungs that he hated his life and that he needed his friend.

Within minutes, the police arrived. You could see the lights coming over the hill. Three cars pulled around him. I quickly ran down the hall and woke up my parents. I pleaded for them to go out and help him.

By the time we got outside, the whole neighborhood was outside. Tommy was on his knees with his hands cuffed behind his back. He was crying. I ran over to give him a hug. The police moved me away. I tried again, but they just would not let me. One of the officers walked me over to my parents.

My dad was talking to an officer. I think he was trying to give the officer a little information about Tommy's background. My dad asked if Tommy could be released into our care. He then walked over to Trevon's family. My dad introduced himself, talked to them and convinced them to drop the charges. They agreed and the officers released Tommy to my family.

My brother was in the house waiting for us to return. He had no desire to be near any police officer. I didn't blame him with all that he'd been through. He was sitting in the living room looking out the window. I guess he was able to follow what was happening by the events he saw take place. He opened the door. We walked in and all went to the living room. My mother ran a warm bath for Tommy. My dad talked to him and hugged him to get him to calm down.

His loud cries turned to sobs within minutes. Tommy walked up the steps to the bathroom. He must have laid in the tub for about forty minutes. My brother brought him a pair of his pajamas, and after Tommy changed clothes, I took him to the guest room and waited for him to get comfortable.

As I started to leave, I heard him say in a low voice, "Please don't leave." I came back and sat in the chair next to his bed. I felt uncomfortable—not because I was around Tommy but because I was thinking about my father's reaction if he knew I was in a room with a boy who wasn't my brother. Then I looked at how peaceful Tommy looked as the moonlight shone on his face. It was like all of his troubles had been lifted. By four o'clock we were both asleep.

I woke up with a kink in my neck. My mother was yelling once again for me to come to breakfast. Tommy was still sleeping. I was able to tiptoe down the hall to my room. Just before I reached it, my dad came out of his room. I thought I was busted, but he just nodded and said, "Good morning." You could see in his face that he knew that sleeping in the guest room was an innocent gesture between friends.

"Hey, Daddy." I gave him a kiss on the cheek, bypassed my room, and went down to eat breakfast. Everyone was quiet. I think we were just tired from all the previous night's activities.

After I ate, I called Damian. I had to tell him about everything that happened after we got off the phone. Of course, I left out the fact that I spent the night in the same room as Tommy. Damian was concerned about us being under the same roof, especially after Tommy had verbally attacked me in the limousine. Damian just didn't trust him anymore. I tried to tell him how "sick" Tommy was. So I broke down and gave him details of what had happened over the last few months. Damian said he understood. But I don't think he was totally convinced. He warned me not to let my guard down.

My dad called us to the living room for a family meeting. I got off the phone with Damian and walked downstairs. My mom, dad, and brother were waiting on me. The looks on their faces concerned me. I knew everything was happening fast, but I had to help my friend who was in need. Apparently my parents had been talking about this through the night.

They told me that the next few months would not be easy. The first thing they needed to do was talk to Tommy's dad. I knew that would be tough because, as far as I knew, Tommy's dad was only into "entertaining" ladies and did not care less about raising his son. He hadn't taken any time to talk to Tommy, especially since Ray's mom had moved away and basketball season was over. His father really didn't care about lacrosse season. What was important now was to get both of them some help.

My dad went to Tommy's house to talk to his dad. He found him just lying on the couch, babbling on and on about Ray's mother. My dad sat next to him and started to talk. My dad told him how Ray's family had moved away and how his son had been wandering around the neighborhood. Tommy's dad sat in silence and then broke down crying. He'd never meant for things to turn out this way.

My dad explained that he could be mad, he could apologize, but regardless, he had to take care of himself and his son. My dad spent most of the day at Tommy's house. By the time he got home, he looked exhausted.

Daddy called Tommy down to have a heart-to-heart talk. Since Tommy was going to stay with us for a few months, he needed to understand the house rules. The main rule was to stay away from my room. He also needed to know that my dad was there if he ever needed to talk.

He told Tommy about his father's condition (physical and mental) and how he needed medical attention. My dad had to be brutally honest with Tommy. He also told him about how his dad's promiscuous behavior had gotten him into this situation that had ruined his family. My father sensed that Tommy had some of the same behaviors and did not want Tommy to follow in the same path.

I decided to call Damian to keep him updated. I figured being honest will put his mind at ease. He sounded concerned about Tommy living in the same house. "That's my boy, but he's smooth. For some reason, girls know all about him, but they are still attracted to him."

"Well, I'm extremely happy with the guy in my life, so I'm not really worried about Tommy."

"Oh, yeah, this guy you like must be realllllllly special."

"He's all right." We both laughed.

Then Tommy walked in and interrupted. He heard Damian and me on the phone. He told me that my mom wanted me for dinner. I told Damian I would call him back. Damian told me how he couldn't wait. I hung up and started walking out the door.

Tommy stopped me and grabbed my hand. He said, "DeDe, thank you for being such a good friend. I've never met any girl like you." Then he moved in like he was going to kiss me.

I put my hand right up to his face and asked, "What in the hell do you think you're doing? I know you are going through some stuff, but I'm not one of the things you are going to go through. And you know I like your boy. So you know you are wrong. Besides, if I tell my family about this stunt you're pulling right now, after my dad and brother take turns beating your tail, my dad's gonna send you right back to the hell hole you came from."

I pushed past him and headed for the stairs. I didn't turn back, but I knew I'd left him there feeling stupid. I saw my brother standing in his doorway. He was smiling and gave me the thumbs-up sign. I knew my brother would always have my back, but now he also knew that some things I could take care of by myself.

I think Tommy got the message. Fortunately he chose the path of respect. We were able to get along as if he was a part of the family.

The last few weeks of school were cool. I was able to complete all my final projects and maintained my high GPA. Tommy drove me to school every day, which was a perk of having him stay at our house. I couldn't believe how many girls were still hatin' on me over this boy. And what was funny was that I still preferred my walks to the bus stop every afternoon … with D.

P.S. A note from the Author

When I first started writing this book, I never knew I had so much to tell. I realized I was funny, liked by some and hated by others, but it took me years to learn my uniqueness is my gift. I always knew I was different, but I never understood my purpose.

This book is filled with stories that occurred in my life. Some are hilarious, others are hard to swallow, and some are a part of my imagination. All were shared to let the world know that everyone's life, with all of the crazy stories, is a gift to the world.

From the time I started writing, it took me ten years to publish plus four additional years to learn to believe in myself and know that I am worthy. It took me all this time to truly love myself exactly how God made me.

And in doing so, I am officially an author, I have the best relationships with my family and friends, and I embrace my uniqueness and smile often. I give back to the world; no matter how small the action, I make a difference. I have the best memories, and I found love.

And you will too …

I love me